The Homesteaders
Reflections

Julian Ashbourn

*To my dear friend Kathy
With Warmest Regards
Julian Ashbourn*

Copyright © 2013 Julian Ashbourn
All rights reserved
ISBN - 13 978 - 1484065013

This book is dedicated to all those who strive in life, only to find that luck is not necessarily on their side. And yet, they retain their sense of proportion, their sense of humour and their fundamental humanity.

Contents

Chapter 1. The Funeral	1
Chapter 2. Early Memories	15
Chapter 3. The Formative Years	29
Chapter 4. A New Direction	47
Chapter 5. The Future Unfolds	63
Chapter 6. A New Life	77
Chapter 7. Changing Times	89
Chapter 8. Reflections	99
Chapter 9. Epilogue	109

Chapter 1. The Funeral

Downtown Montreal on a wet, chilly autumn afternoon can seem very grey and drab. The colours of the store fronts try to break through the gloom but, somehow, they never quite manage the task, the endless grey clouds sweeping across the skies as if in defiance and casting their doleful spell on all around. Nevertheless, I had plenty to do. Having met the elder of my two daughters for lunch and a chat, I now had to rush over to the offices of the Montreal Gazette for whom I had been writing a series of articles as a freelance journalist. It was 1942 with war raging in Europe and nothing but disturbing news hitting the headlines. Consequently, readers appreciated the diversion of the articles I was writing about the natural history of Canada. After that, there was some shopping to do before finally heading home.

A typical day perhaps, except, that all through the day I had an unpleasant feeling that something was wrong. I felt restless and unable to concentrate on matters in the way that I would usually do. My daughter had asked me if everything was all right. "Yes, everything's fine" I replied with a smile, "I'm just a little tired, that's all". It occurred to me that there may be a problem with my articles for the Gazette, or perhaps a friend somewhere was ill. Parking the car in Saint Antoine Street, I made my way to the Montreal Gazette offices and called in on the features editor. Our discussions were brief and good humoured, my articles being well received, and I soon found myself back outside and heading for the car. But the strange feeling of restlessness remained as I closed the door and headed off towards the main shopping centre. Similarly during my shopping where, uncharacteristically, I made several silly mistakes, my mind being seemingly elsewhere. As I approached the car once again, loaded with groceries, it suddenly became clear to me that the source of my concerns was a very special friend of mine who resided back in Saskatchewan, the province in which I was born and raised. My intuition was rarely wrong on such occasions and, as I drove home, I became convinced that this was what had been troubling me. I resolved to telephone long distance to Prince Albert as soon as I arrived back home.

Of course, when I did arrive home, there were a hundred things to attend to, including preparing an evening meal for my husband and myself. Consequently, I did not phone immediately, as I had intended. In fact, to be truthful, I was hesitating to make the call at all, as I was naturally apprehensive as to what I might discover, in spite of my husband urging me to make the call before dinner. However, the matter was taken out of my hands when, just as I was laying the table, the telephone rang. My husband glanced at me, his expression clearly urging me to answer the call. As I lifted the receiver and heard the voice of my friend's son, my heart sank within me and my throat tightened. "I am afraid I have some bad news..." the voice on the other end began. I do not really remember the rest of the conversation, I already knew the purpose of the call. My dear friend had gone. He had passed away, somewhat unexpectedly, earlier that day. There would be a funeral at the little church locally in two days time, and it was hoped that I would manage to get there. Of course I would get there. I must get there. I replaced the receiver and wanted to cry. But I was numb and, in any event, there was no time for tears. I scrambled around and found a train timetable, which indicated that there was an express train west leaving Montreal very early the next morning. If I caught that train, I would be in Moose Jaw or Saskatoon by the early hours of the next morning, and in Prince Albert a couple of hours later. I telephoned my friends in Prince Albert and agreed to meet them there the morning after next, from where we would travel together to the church, around 100 kilometres or so further north. My husband reminded me that we hadn't eaten and that there was still plenty of time to pack. He couldn't accompany me, much as he would have liked to, because he was particularly busy at his place of work, but he would take me to the station in good time and see me safely on the train.

The next morning, I was up at 5.00 and checking my things ready for the journey. After a light breakfast, we drove to the station in my husbands station wagon, with barely a word spoken as we rushed through the deserted streets to the station. Arriving in plenty of time, my husband accompanied me to the ticket office and I purchased an open ended return ticket. After thanking the cashier, I turned to my husband to say goodbye. Suddenly, I was overcome and, for the first time, burst into tears. Could this really be happening? Was I really going to the funeral of one of the dearest and most important friends of my lifetime? Why had he passed away unexpectedly? Why hadn't I troubled to see more of him in recent years? My husband comforted me and reminded me to focus on the journey ahead. I regained my composure and we sat together and waited for the train. It arrived on time, with much clanking and heaving as the big trains do. After fond farewells with my husband, I found my place in the near empty car and settled down to await departure. As the train pulled slowly away, I waved to my husband through the window until he was out of sight and then settled down to rest. Maybe I could even grab a little sleep. I closed my eyes and tried to drift away, but to no avail. Soon the train had gathered speed and was tearing through the countryside, past the lakes and fields of various autumn hues, farms and towns appearing briefly and then vanishing again as though they hadn't really existed at all. After a an hour or two, I went to the refreshment car and had a coffee and a small cake. There were relatively few passengers in the car, presumably most had stayed in their compartments or in the main cars. I went back to my seat and tried to sleep as the train rattled on and on. It would be around nine in the evening before the train would roll into Winnipeg for a scheduled stop, and around five the next morning before arriving in Saskatoon. It was a very long trip and there was nothing to do but relax and try to rest as much as possible. Many thoughts ran through my mind of the old days, my upbringing in Saskatchewan, the friends I had made there and, of course, my dear departed friend.

When the train finally arrived in Saskatoon, I felt very tired and travel weary. No matter, I had to quickly change platforms and get the first train up to Prince Albert where I would meet up with my friends, the

Picards, who once ran the post office there. I arrived at their house on 13th Street East at almost exactly eight in the morning. They welcomed me in and suggested that, as we still had an hour or so before we needed to leave, I take the opportunity to freshen myself up and relax a little. When I came downstairs from the bathroom, a delightful breakfast had been prepared and we enjoyed catching up on old times and renewing our acquaintance. Soon, it was time to leave and we arranged ourselves in the Picard's car, with my luggage in the boot, and moved off towards the bridge over the North Saskatchewan River. Not a great deal had changed since I was last here. The houses were a little nicer perhaps, and the roads a little smoother. There were more stores and certainly more cars on the road, but as we crossed the bridge and headed north, the familiar Saskatchewan scenery brought back a flood of memories. We chatted about nothing in particular in order to pass the time, as if carefully avoiding the subject of where we were headed and why. I knew that my companions were deeply affected by the passing of my friend, just as I was, and that, just like me, they were apprehensive about attending his funeral. As the car rolled along and the town of Prince Albert became wheat fields, interspersed with clumps of woodland under the big, grey autumn sky, my heart seemed to beat increasingly faster. After an hour or so, we crossed the Spruce River and headed west. It would not be long now. There was no conversation as the car wound its way along the road towards the Sturgeon River junction. And then, in the distance, the little church became visible. It was the same church where, just a few months earlier, this man's best friend had also been laid to rest. There were already a few cars pulled up outside, and people had gathered around the entrance. As we approached, Alexander said simply, "We are here now". We pulled up next to the other cars, and I felt tense and hollow inside as I stepped out from the car and looked towards the church. My friend's widow spotted us straight away and stood serenely watching as we approached. I went up to her and looked into her eyes, as I had done so many times in the past. They seemed sad, but stoically resigned to the realities of life and death. She embraced me and, as we hugged each other, she whispered, "We have both lost him now, my dear. He is gone from this world". The son and his wife came and paid their respects, as did the neighbours to the south and west of them and there was quite a little gathering of people as the service began in the church, where the casket was placed on a table, overlain with a large purple drape. One or two favourite hymns were sung, rather quietly I felt, and then we filed outside for the burial itself, the widow and myself arm in arm as we followed the Reverend, the others behind us. As we stood at the grave-side, I was reminded of a poem once shown to me by a friend. It was called, The Journey.

The journey starts with pain and tears
And heartache in those tender years
Until such times as dreams are sown
And cast against the great unknown

And so the path of life unwinds
Through rain and sun and treasured times
Round towards a future earned
And back again to lessons learned

And on to where we see the light
But not the way we thought we might
For in the dawning of the day
Dreams, once blossomed, fade away

And then, when all is said and done
Beneath the slowly setting sun
We yearn to find a trusted friend
To lead us to the journey's end

And then something unexpected and quite magical occurred. Another car pulled up, and then another. More people were arriving from prince Albert and the surrounding area. There were representatives from the Dominion Lands Office, the Bank, the General Store, and other institutions in the town. And then another car arrived with some sisters from The Academy of Notre Dame de Sion. Others arrived from farms in the area and soon, to our astonishment, the gathering had more than doubled in size. I placed my arm around the widow and, for the first time, felt her tremble as she looked around at all those who had come to say their last goodbye to her beloved husband. As we watched, two large pick up trucks came down the road from the north, each of which contained a number of individuals, both packed into the cabs and in the rear beds. I knew straight away that they were Cree, who had travelled all the way from the Montreal Lake reserve. They were a mixture of ages from elderly to quite young and they filed silently to the other side of the grave and stood watching solemnly. Some of them noticed me and nodded gently, almost imperceptibly. The small gathering had now become a sizable crowd, and yet all were absolutely silent. For a little while, the grey skies parted just enough to bathe the scene in a subdued autumn glow. The Reverend Carter completed the service with a prayer and the casket was lowered into the grave. A handful of dirt was thrown in and the widow shuddered as it hit the casket. I held her arm tightly as the Reverend completed the service and we filed slowly back to assemble at the entrance to the church. One by one, the assembled mourners came up slowly to pay their respects and offer a few comforting words to the widow as they gently took her hand. I instinctively looked over towards the grave. The Cree were still standing there. One of the elders was reciting something with his arms outstretched over the open grave, while the others stood, completely motionless, as if carved from rock. I looked at the widow. She nodded to me and smiled and I went back over to the grave. The elder unwrapped a cloth bundle and produced a large eagle's feather and a beaded cloth. He knelt with one knee on the ground and threw these carefully on to the top of the casket. He then rose and threw in a handful of dirt while whispering some more words. He had noticed me and beckoned me to his side, where he gave me a handful of dirt to throw in afterwards. I did so and, slowly, one at a time, all the Indians came forward in silence and did the same thing. By now, some of the others had started to leave and it was time for the Indians to come and pay their respects to the widow. The elders approached quietly and, one by one, took her hand and spoke to her gently in Cree. The others stood by in silence, their sad eyes fixed upon the widow.

The Indians took their leave and, after a while, just a small group remained. The widow, her son and daughter in law, the Picards, the Kankkunens from the west, the Johanssens from the south and myself. It was agreed that I would stay with the widow for a few days. The others would drop by from time to time to ensure that everything was OK. As we returned slowly to the house, we started to talk more freely and marvelled at the number of people who had appeared, as if from nowhere, to pay their last respects to the deceased. How did they even know about the funeral? But then news travels fast out here on the prairie.

Who was this man, who had attracted such a large and diverse crowd to his funeral, here in the middle of nowhere? What kind of a man could he have been? Actually, he was a simple homesteader and carpenter who lived up on a clearing by the river and his name was John Wilks. And yet, he was in many ways a most remarkable man, much loved within the community which, indeed, he had done so much to create. He came to Canada from Newcastle in England, back in 1897 under the provisions of The Homestead Act and, like many others, struggled to establish himself on this sometimes unforgiving land. But he persevered and

The Funeral

made friends easily, and not just with the other settlers. He developed a special friendship with the local Woodlands Cree and devoted a great deal of time and energy to help liaise between themselves and the authorities in order to ensure that their needs were met as they abandoned their traditional camps and moved to the reserve further north. This was a friendship which endured throughout his life and which was nurtured by both sides. Indeed, his widow, Kanti was a Cree Indian and they had enjoyed a very happy life together in the house that he had himself built by the river. John Wilks was known and respected throughout the northern half of the province for his kindness and integrity. He was a modest man who, nonetheless, left an indelible impression on the lives of many in the area. I know because I am one of them.

And me? My name is Kimi Anderson. These days, I live in a beautiful house in a quiet area of Montreal with my husband Eric, and have two lovely daughters who visit us regularly. My husband is a senior engineer with Canadian Pacific and I am a part time journalist, writing articles for the primary newspapers and magazines in Montreal. I must say that we live a very comfortable life and have everything we need in that delightful city. But my life used to be very different. You see, I am also a full blood Cree Indian. I might yet be on the reserve up at Montreal Lake had it not been for the influence of this very dear man. A man who came into my life at a time when it, quite literally, hung in the balance.

I was not quite five years of age, living with my parents and elder brother, for most of the year, in a one room cabin nestled in the woods, far to the north of where John Wilks had settled. Like many small children in our community, I had become sick and was in the grip of a terrifying fever. It was clear that, without help, I would die. Indeed, my parents told me later that they were resigned to losing me. And then, a friend of my fathers whose name was Etchemin, the son of a chief, told him about a young Englishman who he had met and become friends with, down in a clearing by the Sturgeon River. He thought that this man might know how to help me. My parents, by now desperate, were prepared to try anything and so, I was bundled up in a blanket and, together with Etchemin and one or two others, they made their way down the trail, through the woods and, eventually, out into the clearing, beyond which the prairie stretched out towards the south. I remember little about the journey, except when I was brought into a strange cabin, later that day, and laid down upon a raised structure which I later came to know as a bed. I looked around me and wondered where we were and why we had come here. Etchemin was speaking with someone in English, a language of which I knew but a few words. This stranger had his back to me and then, turned around and knelt down by the bed. He looked down at me and took my hand in his and then placed his other hand, very gently, upon my forehead. I looked up at him and our eyes locked together. In that moment, I knew that he was a friend. A very special friend, who, in my childish innocence, I reasoned, had been sent especially to look after me. Perhaps it was because I was not used to seeing brown eyes, but I couldn't take my eyes off him and held his gaze until he rose and started to talk with Etchemin and my parents again. I watched, weak but fascinated, as he built up the fire in his cabin and placed

The Funeral

a pot on the cooking grid. A little while later, he came to the bedside again with a bowl and a spoon and, propping me up on his pillows, started to feed me with a hot broth. I gazed into his face as he slowly fed me, a small spoonful at a time, and then laid me back down and covered me carefully with a blanket. Some further discussion took place. I didn't really understand it and, now feeling warm and comfortable, drifted in and out of sleep. And then, my father, Etchemin and the others left, leaving my mother and this stranger with me in the cabin. Some more broth was prepared and the stranger fed me a little more, before discussing something with my mother. It looked as though he was preparing a bed for her by the fire and then, he came over and knelt by the bed I was lying in and gently took my hand as he looked to see if I was all right. I opened my eyes again and looked into those kindly brown eyes. He smiled at me, and I felt as though I already knew him from somewhere. I gripped his hand as tightly as I could under the circumstances, and he, very gently, turned and sat by the bed without letting go of my hand. Exhausted by the journey and warmed by the broth, I quickly fell into a deep sleep. When I awoke, it was morning, and that dear man was still sitting there, holding my hand.

I quickly remembered the events of the previous day, and that I was in a strange cabin with my mother and this stranger. My mother came and looked at me and asked me, in Cree, how I was feeling now. I whispered that I felt a little better. The man disappeared outside for a while and then came back in and came over to me. He smiled and said some words as he gently placed his hand on my forehead again. I didn't quite understand the language, but I understood his meaning perfectly. He made me some more broth and came over to feed me again. I gleefully sat up and looked into his kindly face as he fed me a spoon at a time. My mother came over and told him my name. "Kimi?" he said, followed by some more words in English which I took to understand that he liked the name. He smiled and spoke my name again, very softly. A bond had been created between us which would not be broken until death itself intervened.

The Funeral

Chapter 2. Early Memories

My earliest memories are of living in a one room cabin with my parents and elder brother, Keme, who always seemed to be away with other children from our small community. We were at a pleasant site by a small river which wound its way through the woods and there was always something interesting to explore. I loved to watch the animals who would sometimes roam through the woods. There were caribou and elk and often, at night, we would hear the wolves, although I seldom saw them. There were also bears, which we did see from time to time, although they were quite shy. The red squirrels and birds were, by contrast, not the least bit shy and were always around the cabin. I used to feed them little titbits which my mother would give to me as she was preparing meals. The animals, the river and the forest were all an integral part of our life and, except during the winter, I spent most of my time outside, playing and exploring and chatting to my animal friends, who always responded, either in sounds or body language. I never thought of animals as inferior species. They were simply our friends and neighbours in the forest. We had no furniture as such in our cabin, but each of us had a corner where we would keep our own things tidy and, at night, we made our beds with blankets, fur rugs and home made pillows. Most of the cooking was done outside, unless the weather was bad, in which case, there was a fire place at one end of the cabin where we could heat food if required. As the winter approached, my parents would start gathering their things together and the community would start, on foot, on a long journey south. It was very tiring for a small child, but I was also fascinated by all the areas we would pass through and the transition from the forest to the sparse woodlands and, eventually, the open plains. After what seemed like several days of walking, we would finally set up camp by the side of a big lake, with a surface like glass, and often spend the evenings around a large fire which all the families would contribute to. The sparks from the fire would drift upwards until they disappeared somewhere under a canopy of a million stars, all sparkling brightly in the night sky. We had meat and shrubs which the men provided while the women attended to the camp. I never knew from where they got such provisions, but the men went out most every day and always came back with something. The evening meals, in the cool late autumn air, were always eagerly anticipated and enjoyed with a relish.

There was always a degree of interaction with the various Europeans in the area at that time, mostly for the purposes of trade. We would supply surplus furs, skins and items made in the camp, and they would supply tools, pots and other goods. The concept of money was not strong at that time, but the art of trading was well developed and the men in the camp prided themselves on their negotiating skills, as well as their hunting ability. Most of the men understood and spoke English, at least to some degree, and some of them a little French as well, although we met fewer Frenchmen out here on the prairies. The children, including myself, would enjoy picking up a few English words and using them within our playful intercourse. From the lake, we also obtained fish and I often sat with my mother while she prepared and dried the fish or was otherwise engaged in preparing a meal of some kind. At such times, she would often sing to me in her quiet, gentle voice and I was never happier than sitting by the lakeside with my mother in the winter sunshine, with the camp bustling around us. In those days, we had no concept of being rich or poor. We were simply alive, and living in harmony with nature in our beautiful world. Sometimes, of course, things wouldn't go according to plan and our provisions ran low, but we would always scrape through. Our worst fear was illness. If there was a fever going around, it was difficult to understand or predict its consequences. Mostly, those affected would recover, but sometimes they did not. As I child, I struggled to understand why people, especially other children, were lost in this way, and I wondered where their souls had gone to, and why. There were various tales of spirits crossing huge lakes and finding a secret place where they could live for ever more in peace. Or travelling up through the sky to the stars, or maybe coming back again as eagles, or bears. I simply imagined a secret place, somewhere in a beautiful forest with a river running through it, and where the spirits of all good people would go and be happy.

And there were stories. Always stories. The Cree are natural story tellers. It is part of their heritage and ingrained in almost every individual. In the evenings, it would be usual to gather around the camp fire and, after summary discussions of the day's events, someone or other would start a story and everyone would listen attentively as the tale unfolded. Some of the stories were traditional tales that, while familiar in their primary structure, would often be embellished slightly by the individual telling them. Others would be intuitively constructed on the spot, perhaps inspired by a hunting episode or other event of the day. And some were sacred stories that needed to be properly told and were entrusted mostly to the elders. Some stories became firmly associated with an individual and regarded as their personal property. They would refine and embellish them to a point of high artistic merit, and would take great pride, and care, in their telling. I would listen to the stories and they would create their own image in my mind's eye, and stay with me, just as, later on in my life, reading a good book would create a similar impression. You might say that the Cree had a library of such stories, and it was a rich and extensive library, passed down from generation to generation. But of course, my favourite stories were those told to me by my parents. Mostly my mother, but occasionally by my father who would take great care to sit down with me somewhere and slowly unravel a tale with great deliberation.

Our winter camps brought a seasonal change of lifestyle which was both familiar and refreshing. When the leaves started to turn colour in the autumn, I would already be looking forward to the winter camp, the beautiful lake, fish, and stories around the fire. With the spring melt, we would travel back to our camp in the woods and it was always a joyful homecoming as we cleaned and prepared the cabin and returned to our usual routine. I would immediately renew my acquaintance with many of the animals in the woods and on the banks of the river, always finding something new and interesting in the natural world. Our life was simple, but those early years were happy times and I enjoyed those first years of life. After my illness, things started to change. I had now been introduced to Europeans in a way in which I never expected. Up until then, all I knew of Europeans is that they would appear, almost out of nowhere, and trade with the men of our band, before disappearing again, sometimes not to be seen for months. There had been much talk within our community of settlers. Those who came and stayed on the land, planting crops and farming. At first, this was a curiosity, but quickly became a concern due to their numbers and how they were changing the land. However, up until that time, I had never even seen a settler or had any idea what they were like and what they did. And then, fate decreed that I was to meet John Wilks. The impression he made upon me was immediate and deep. We became soul mates straight away and were able to communicate, not so much as adult and child, although he was always very protective of me, but as true friends. We both enjoyed and appreciated the natural world and were comfortable in each others company. As our relationship developed, I would refer to him, when speaking with others, as my uncle John. In our community, the relationship between niece or nephew and uncle, was an important and respected one. However, between ourselves, it was always just John and Kimi and we spoke freely together on almost everything. But I am jumping ahead. This relationship took a while to develop fully as, as soon as I was on the road to recovery, my mother and I returned to our cabin in the woods and only saw John occasionally, when he would come to talk with the other men or, rarely, when we would make the journey south. But whenever he was around, we quickly got together and, typically, I would be by his side the whole time, either listening to the wider conversation or, to my delight, being alone with him as we walked by the banks of the river and chatted together.

My very early years passed by quickly and I found myself growing up with the twin influences of my own, dear parents within our community, and John Wilks. I quickly perfected my English and John painstakingly taught me to read and write in English and introduced me to the wonder of books, via the handful he had managed to collect together in his cabin. This collection grew steadily in those years and he was always on the lookout for any interesting book, which he would take great pleasure in introducing to me, often while chatting by the fireside in his newly built house. And, of course, sometimes he would acquire a book as a special gift for me. In my corner of our family cabin, among my collection of special stones and other personal treasures, I would give pride of place to my tiny collection of well worn second hand books, of which my favourite was a very worn copy of David Copperfield, which had some pages missing, although, to me, this simply added to the mystique. Through these, and John himself, I was learning that there was a whole world beyond the confines of our Cree community and, to an inquisitive child, it seemed like a wonderful and magical world. Furthermore, if all Europeans were like John, then they couldn't be as bad as some in our community feared. Naturally, I was to learn later that all Europeans were not necessarily like John Wilks. But these were exciting days for a young child, with a wonderful world around me and so much going on, both within our community and beyond. Significant events over the next few years were to shape my character and plot my destiny in a way which was hardly expected.

In the year following John Wilks' arrival in Saskatchewan, he became very ill himself, having contracted a bad fever. Fortunately, he had already befriended our band and when this was discovered, his friends Etchemin and Chogan made arrangements for him to be cared for. This was largely undertaken by the daughter of one of the most respected elders, whose name was Kanti. She nursed John back to the point at which he could once again fend for himself and, during this brief period, a close friendship developed between them. From then on, whenever they happened to meet, they were drawn ever more closer together. It was understood that John expected his sweetheart from England to come and join him once he had become properly established. However, Kanti always had a different understanding and was confident that, one day, she and John would be united as husband and wife. And so the weeks passed by and then, unexpectedly, John heard that his sweetheart from England would not be joining him after all. In our community, we all waited patiently as we knew that it was only a matter of time before John and Kanti would get together. Eventually, the inevitable occurred and a date was set for a wedding. In fact, two weddings, as they were to have both a Christian wedding and a traditional Cree wedding the next day. I was around five and a half years of age at this time and eagerly awaited the event as I knew that my uncle John would invite me along with the other guests. The Christian wedding took place at John's house, to which a group of friends had been invited, together with the preacher who had travelled up from Prince Albert. I travelled down with my parents and some of John's friends from our band, including the elders, who were curious to see the ceremony. I remember that, when we arrived, everyone seemed to be bustling about in preparation. Odile Picard, the lady from the Post Office in Prince Albert seemed to be organising everything and others were helping as best they could. There was a strange Frenchman who was one of John's friends, who I believe was named Jacques and, a very kind lady whom I had already met in Prince Albert by the name of Margaret Sim. I knew that John was very fond of Margaret, and so I went up to her and, as usual, she was very attentive and kind to me. Kanti looked very beautiful, but the service was over quite quickly and people fell into chatting together about many things. John chatted with his Indian friends and, to my delight, came over to me and suggested that we take a little walk by the river while the others were talking. He spoke to me gently about marriage and how important it was, and then he said, as if reassuring me, that I would always be welcome to come and stay with him and Kanti whenever I wanted to, subject of course to my parent's approval. I was overjoyed as I knew that I would have a lovely time in their company and enjoy being by the river in that beautiful spot where his house was located. He also had a horse that I could ride and his workshop which was full of interesting things.

The next day, we moved back north to where our cabins were situated and joined the community there in preparations for the Cree wedding which would take place the next day. Bride and groom stayed separately, John with Etchemin and his family and Kanti with her father and relatives. The next day, they participated in the Cree wedding and were presented with various gifts including some ceremonial moccasins which my mother had made. We all wondered how John would react to the ceremony, but he took to it as though he himself was a Cree Indian and everyone was happy. There was a great feast afterwards and many small gifts were exchanged, even with some individuals from other bands who had heard about the wedding and travelled from further north or east to join us. It was a very happy occasion and I stayed close to John throughout. Many times, he looked down at me and took my hand in his for a few moments. By now, he was considered my surrogate uncle by all in our band, and everyone seemed pleased with this development. Now that he was married to Kanti, the bond became even stronger. The next morning, when it was time for them to return home, I was very sad and knew that I would miss them terribly. But there would be visits to and fro, and, as promised, John and Kanti allowed me to go and stay with them for several days at a time, and these would be very happy times. Kanti was more than an auntie to me, she was like a big sister who always advised me properly and took great care of me when I was with them. And John, of course, was wonderful, taking me for walks by the river, where we would discuss all manner of things, quietly and gently. We observed all the different life forms by the river and I would sometimes make up stories which John always enjoyed. Sometimes, I would watch him in his workshop and he showed me how to fashion simple objects out of wood. We would often make little ornaments, either for Kanti or my parents and John always insisted that I had made them, even though, in truth, we had made them together. They were happy days and I realised how lucky I was to have my two families. John would worry sometimes that he was taking me away from my parents, but this was not the case at all. I loved and respected my mother and father deeply and they were pleased that I also had John and Kanti as my uncle and aunt. Sometimes we would all be together and I was never happier than on those occasions.

And such was our life under the big skies and prairie moon, which might have continued that way, except, more and more people were arriving in Saskatchewan to take advantage of the Homestead Act. John explained this to me, but, at that time, I didn't understand why people would want to come and change the land in the way that they did. Among our community, this became a point of contention and many of the elders were not happy with the situation. They considered John a friend and as one of their own, but they did not enjoy the same relationship with most of the settlers, and certainly not with those in the town of Prince Albert. There was no actual hostility on either side, but an underlying suspicion that their land and their life was being changed significantly by the influx of settlers and that things would never be the same again. It was a complex situation as the government sought to divide up the land and keep areas free for the Indians. There was much discussion on this point within our band and, eventually, it was decided that we would also move onto the reserve up at Montreal Lake. My parents explained to me that this would be for the best as we were to be given better cabins and facilities such as proper health care. I learned that, in the background, John was doing everything he could to negotiate with the Department of Indian Affairs on our behalf and ensure that we were treated properly and given everything that was due to us.

He never mentioned this to me himself, but this was typical of him. He simply did what he considered was the right thing to do, without any thought of self promotion or reward.

And so we moved to the reserve at Montreal Lake. It was true that we were given much better cabins to live in. Ours was large, divided internally into three large rooms, with proper glazed windows and a well fitted door with a lock, something we had never used before. It also had a proper kitchen and cooking area with a range and a sink, divided off from the larger room. My mother was pleased with the cabin and set about decorating it with various bits and pieces. The two smaller rooms were used as bedrooms, one of which I shared with my brother, although he always seemed to be somewhere else. However, Montreal Lake was very different from the small community we were used to. There were so many people, and they were not all friendly towards us. Among the other children, some of the older boys were noisy and seemed aggressive. I didn't enjoy being with them and, consequently, spent most of my time with my parents or alone. The lake itself was beautiful, with woods stretching out around its northern shores, but it was not as interesting as our previous location. There were few trails within the woods and those that did exist were often busy with people moving around. I felt that there was no secluded place where I could enjoy the natural world as I used to, or talk to the animals and lose myself in my private thoughts. After a while, I noticed a change in my parents and others of our band, who became somewhat withdrawn and, increasingly, kept themselves to themselves, except during important meetings. This was not how it used to be and I didn't really like it there.

In truth, with all those extra people around me, I was lonely. Lonely and unhappy. It brings to mind another little poem which my friend showed to me once, called Somewhere.

> Somewhere in the darkest night
> A light is burning
> Somewhere in the coldest heart
> A flame appears
> Down through all the broken dreams
> The world keeps turning
> Every little new born hope
> Is bathed in tears
>
> Somewhere in the rolling sea
> A voice is calling
> Somewhere on a distant shore
> A heart cries out
> Somewhere in a far off sky
> A star is falling
> Somewhere in the dark
> A little hand is reaching out
>
> Somewhere in the wind
> A soul is searching
> Somewhere in the mist
> A love lies lost
> Somewhere far away
> A heart is hurting
> Somewhere on the path
> A hope lies tossed

> And when the healing starts
> And time begins once more
> Hearts will fly free
> From all the weight they bore
> Rising to the skies
> With swallows song they'll soar

The first time that I visited John and Kanti after moving to the reserve, John realised that something was wrong and we went for a little walk by the river to chat. When I explained to him how different things were at Montreal lake, he reassured me that things will probably take a little time to settle down and that it will get better. But at his house by the river, all those cares seemed to quickly evaporate and I enjoyed being in their company once again. John had been campaigning to establish a proper school up on the reserve and, while the proposal had been accepted and the initial structure was built, it was proving difficult to get equipment and, most of all, a properly qualified teacher. It seemed that no one was interested in moving to this out of the way spot in northern Saskatchewan. And then, on a subsequent visit to my favourite house by the river, something happened that, once again, was to have a big impact upon my life. John's untiring efforts on our behalf had finally borne fruit and a teacher had been found. What was more, she was scheduled to travel to John's house, after which he would escort her north to the reserve. As I was staying with them at that time, I would also travel home with John and the new teacher. Actually, I was rather apprehensive as I had little idea of what a proper teacher was like and I imagined a fairly authoritative and stern figure. John reassured me that this was not the case and that I would get along very well with this person. I trusted his judgment of course, but was still a little nervous about meeting the teacher. On the appointed day we waited expectantly and then, in the middle afternoon, saw a carriage approaching from the south. John's friend from the Dominion Lands Office was bringing the teacher up from Prince Albert. As they drew nearer, I could see a nice looking lady in a flowing dress and large hat and was intrigued to think that this was the teacher. On arrival, John helped her from the carriage and, immediately, she came over to me and asked who I was. "This is Kimi, your new star pupil" John explained in a serious tone. The teacher looked into my eyes for a moment, and then a broad smile spread across her face. "Well, I am very pleased to meet you Kimi, you must tell me all about your family and the reserve". I liked her straight away, and we went into the house together to meet Kanti. The teacher's name was Sarah Campbell and she was an attractive looking Metis woman who had been educated in the east but was originally from Saskatchewan. She understood the local position very well and assured me that, with my help, we would create a lovely school up on the reserve. Suddenly, I felt much better about Montreal Lake.

Chapter 3. The Formative Years

Staying with my uncle John and Kanti had represented a highlight of my existence at that time and I always looked forward to the next trip south, my walks by the river and all the interesting things that were to be found in and around their house which, to me, was the most beautiful house in the world. Actually, it was a simply constructed stone structure with inset wooden windows and doors and a conventional tiled roof. But it had tremendous character, partly no doubt due to the loving care with which John had created it, with some help from his friends and neighbours, including at one point, his Cree friends. It was as though it had a little of all those individuals embedded into its ragged stone walls. Inside, the walls had been smoothed and plastered with a mix of clay and then painted which, when the light shone through the windows, tended to illuminate every room. But it was Kanti's touch which really turned it into a home, and a beautiful home at that. Over time, she decorated it with a mix of beautiful woven fabrics inspired by the Cree traditions, and ornaments, some of which John had made and some which she herself had constructed. It was a treasure trove of interesting items, bright colours and, most of all, a house filled with love. Indeed, it was interesting to note how many people came and went whenever I was there. Anyone travelling south to north or vice versa would seem to call in at the Wilks house, the door of which, in the summer at least, was always open. And of course, John's neighbours and friends the Kankkunens, the Haajanens, the Turners, and later the Johanssens always seemed to be stopping by, even though it meant quite a journey for them. I got to know all of these people, who seemed to regard me almost as John and Kanti's daughter and were never surprised to find me there.

John's closest friend was Veijo Kankkunen whom he had met on the ship coming over from England. Veijo had a wife named Anja and two small children, Keke and Virpi, with whom John naturally got along very well. In fact, he told me that it was Keke who had actually brought them together on the ship when he was lost and John helped him find his parent's cabin. They had no idea at that stage that they would eventually end up as neighbours out on the prairie. When they discovered this, they were overjoyed of course and spent many happy times together. However, their happiness was turned to grief later on when, as sometimes happened in those early days, a fever swept its way across the land and took poor little Virpi. Veijo was to tell me, many years later, that it was then that John showed his true colours as a loyal and sympathetic friend, helping them when they most needed it, to deal with the practicalities and to come to terms with their loss. Although, also like many, I don't think they ever did get over the loss of little Virpi. Certainly, Veijo grieved for her for the rest of his days and Keke, although he never said much, was clearly affected by the loss of his little sister. Perhaps, in a way, that is why Keke and I always got along well together. He was four years older, and I think I was, in some way at least, a surrogate sister for him. He was also a brother for me as, although I had my brother Keme, I actually saw little of him as he was always running around with the other boys on the reserve and rarely at home. Back on the reserve, I was sometimes teased about my going to stay with John and Kanti, but I didn't mind as I knew how lucky I was to have this extended family, from whom I learned so much. Of course, once we had moved to the reserve at Montreal Lake, it was more difficult to travel back and forth and my trips became fewer.

Having met Sarah Campbell at the Wilks house, the next morning, we all set off together for Montreal Lake. I had already been asking Miss Campbell a thousand questions about the school and what we would study there. She was extremely patient and explained to me all the things that she would like to introduce but, of course, she hadn't even seen the school house at that point. The journey north was filled with conversation and laughter as we discussed many things about the area, the reserve and the new school. Miss Campbell had already promised that she would let me help with setting up the school and arranging things locally and I was looking forward to it all accordingly. When we arrived back at the reserve, John introduced Sarah Campbell to everyone and carried her things into the school house. My parents wanted me to stay at home, but I was much too interested in all that was going on and followed John around everywhere. Having got Sarah Campbell settled, John took me to our cabin and then went off to stay with Etchemin, promising me that he would come and collect me in the morning. I was restless all night and felt instinctively that the school was now going to play a big part in my life. The next morning, I went with John to the school house where Miss Campbell had already made her appraisal of the situation and had started on a list of additional things that she would need. John set up a couple of black boards for her and helped her wherever he could. She explained to me that the school wasn't yet open but that I could stay and help her if I wanted to. Of course, I did want to and we quickly struck up a friendship, although I was always somewhat in awe of her as a teacher. I helped organise the work books and we made a list of children who we thought would attend. Miss Campbell also mentioned that she would need some adult volunteers to help with things and I promised to speak with my parents about this. John returned home that day and, the next morning, the school opened. To Miss Campbell's surprise, it seemed that almost all the children had heard about the school and wanted to attend. Space was clearly going to be a problem. But we started off and, immediately, I loved every moment and always stayed after the classes were finished in order to help Miss Campbell and chat about the lessons. In this way, I was able to discuss anything that I hadn't quite understood and, very quickly, I was gaining confidence and developing a thirst for knowledge. The school's facilities were basic and there were not enough books and materials to go around at first, but this slowly improved, thanks in large part to John who worked tirelessly as a liaison with the Department of Indian Affairs. Local women helped on a rota basis with the basic organisational tasks and, in fact, it was quite some time before we got another couple of teachers.

The school and, especially, Sarah Campbell, made a very big impression upon me. Now I had something to look forward to every day and something to keep me occupied. Just as John had predicted, things seemed to be improving on the reserve. During the school holiday periods, I would go to stay with John and Kanti for a while and proudly tell them all I had learned. They usually had at least a couple of new books each time I visited and, in the evenings, I would sit with John and we would go through them while Kanti busied herself in the kitchen. During the day, we would go walking by the river, usually just John and myself, although sometimes Kanti would join us. We would talk about the natural world, the situation with the local farmers, the reserve, the school, England, and all manner of things. Looking back on those days, I realise now just how important those discussions were to my overall development. They provided the opportunity for me to test my knowledge and understanding away from the school and among friends, something which few children of my age were able to do. John, in particular, was an inspiration to me, always coming up with new ideas and always explaining to me how things worked and why certain things were important. In parallel, Kanti was like a big sister and taught me all I needed to know about being a woman and human relationships and, of course, my parents taught me all about our heritage and how things worked in our community. All in all, I had a most comprehensive upbringing. But it was the school that really changed my life at this juncture. It instilled in me a love of learning which I was never to loose. My friend had a little verse about learning.

Life is for learning
And learning and learning
Not for regrets
Or unfulfilled yearning

Our days fly away
Like leaves on the wind
But only the truth
Will here remain pinned

And so we must listen
To all that has passed
And not be distracted
By that which can't last

For when we lay down
On our final bed
Our truth will sustain us
In what lies ahead

And so I entered upon a new phase of my life. I knew not what I would do in later years, or where I would be. But I knew that I must learn all I could from the wonderful people who surrounded me. I read whatever books I could find to read and I discussed them with Miss Campbell and, when the opportunity arose, with my uncle John. My parents encouraged me greatly in this, even though it was very different from their own upbringing. I now realise how visionary and how unselfish they were, and I love them all the more for it. They could easily have restricted me to a life on the reserve, and to follow in their own footsteps, but they didn't. I think they realised that there was significant change in the air and that I would need to cultivate a broader perspective if I were to get on in life.

The next few years passed very quickly and the school went from strength to strength. My time was spent studying, helping Miss Campbell, being with my parents and, whenever I could, visiting John and Kanti. John had started to ask me what I knew about other schools and what I thought I wanted to do with my life when I was an adult. I explained that I thought I would like to write books, just like those which I had enjoyed reading so much myself. When we were out walking, he would occasionally slip in some question or other about what subjects I was most interested in, or which books I was studying at the moment. I knew that he was plotting something on my behalf, although I had no idea what. This was very like John Wilks. He was always looking to do something for those around him. He had already done much to improve the situation on the reserve and was highly regarded by the elders and his many friends there. Similarly, I understood, with his friends in Prince Albert. But what could he possibly be planning for me? And why?

My curiosity was answered one bight summer day when he was visiting the reserve. I noticed that he had deliberately spoken with Miss Campbell, my parents and others, without me being present. This was most unusual and a sign that I was the subject of their conversation. Of course, I knew that any such discussion would be around my own welfare and so I waited patiently until we were all together in Etchemin's cabin. Here, John announced that he had been speaking with the Sisters at The Academy of Notre Dame de Sion, a special school for young ladies in Prince Albert, and he thought there was a possibility that they might be persuaded to accept me there as a student. After all, he argued, I had been doing exceptionally well at the school on the reserve and it would be nice to ensure that my education could continue along proper lines. I was delighted and excited by the idea. My parents were worried that they might lose me forever if I went to Prince Albert and others voiced similar concerns. I surely belonged on the reserve with our Cree community. John looked at me across the cabin and, after reading my thoughts, smiled and then reiterated all the reasons why I should go to prince Albert. If I were accepted by the school, he had already arranged for my accommodation and would personally ensure that I had everything I needed for my studies. Furthermore, he would transport me back and forth during the school holidays, so I would be back frequently. To my surprise, it was my father who resolved the issue. He suggested that my mother and I would join him to discuss the matter in our own cabin and would then give John our answer. We left the others and went to our cabin where, my tearful mother hugged me closely. After a minute or two, my father took both of us by the hand and announced quietly that it was best that I should go to Prince Albert if John could arrange it. My mother simply nodded and we returned to Etchemin's cabin where, with various provisos about bringing me straight home if I didn't like it there, it was agreed that I should return with John, who would take me to the Academy to be interviewed by the Sisters.

The trip back down to John's house was filled with conversation about The Academy of Notre Dame, the Sisters and what I might learn there. I think John was as enthusiastic as I was about the prospect of me attending the academy and we discussed how I should present myself at the interview. While apprehensive about the prospect of the interview itself, strangely enough, I had no doubt that I would be accepted and was already thinking about life in Prince Albert. John had already arranged for me to stay with Odile and Alexander Picard at the Post Office, should I be accepted at the academy. I was very pleased with this suggestion as I liked Odile very much and was sure that we would all get along well. We stopped for the night at John's house, where Kanti prepared a lovely meal for us and, to my surprise and delight, had also made a new dress for me to wear at the interview. She was also very excited about this new development and told me that she wished that she had had such an opportunity. We talked into the evening, until John suggested that I should get to bed as the next day would be very busy. I did so, although I slept little that night. Early the next morning, after a light breakfast, we waved goodbye to Kanti and set off south for Prince Albert. Once or twice on the journey and between conversation, I glanced across at John as he was driving the buggy and wondered how it was that I was travelling to Prince Albert with this man who was not from our community and yet was doing so much for me. I marvelled at my good fortune in meeting and becoming friends with him as, suddenly, my position came into a clear focus and I realised that my life was taking an important new direction.

After stopping by at the Post Office to refresh ourselves after the journey, we went over to the Academy of Notre Dame de Sion and met with Mother Elsa and the Sisters. Mother Elsa was a stern looking, but kindly lady who looked deep into my eyes and questioned me as to why I wanted to attend the Academy. After a while, she called in one of the Sisters, who took me to another room to test me on my basic skills of literacy and arithmetic, leaving John with Mother Elsa. I wondered what they were discussing while I was undergoing the tests, but knew that John would be making a good case for me. The test over, Sister Sandrine escorted me back to Mother Elsa's little office without saying a word, simply smiling serenely as she opened the door for me. She handed a note to Mother Elsa and departed, leaving the three of us together. Mother Elsa glanced at the note, and then at John, and then, rather intently, at me. After a pause, as though considering something in her own mind, she smiled and announced that they would be happy to welcome me to the Academy. There were some formalities to undertake and some forms to complete, which John dutifully took care of. My own mind was racing with thoughts of living in Prince Albert and attending the Academy - a school where I was sure that I would learn a great deal. We returned to the Post Office and celebrated with a nice meal and coffee. Odile was delighted as she had already prepared an upstairs room for me, overlooking the street, and John had bought various notebooks, pencils and pens for me, as well as one or two books, which I found waiting for me in the room. They clearly had no doubt that I would be accepted by the school. For the first time in my life, I found myself at a loss for words. I didn't know how to thank both the

Wilks and the Picards for all their kindness towards me. I realised how extraordinarily lucky I was to find myself in such a position. When it came time for John to leave, we went outside to see him off, and, as he adjusted the buggy, he stopped and looked into my eyes with an inquiring gaze. "Are you sure you will be OK Kimi?" he asked. I assured him that I would be more than OK and he reiterated that, if I ever became unhappy, he would come and take me home again. He then hugged me tightly for a moment or two before climbing up on the buggy and rolling away as we waved enthusiastically. Returning inside the Post Office, it felt strange for a while, as I appreciated the significant change in my circumstances, but Odile was absolutely wonderful and made me feel very welcome. I was still somewhat in a daze, with everything happening so quickly and, that night, when I finally settled into my new bed, I wept. Not out of any apprehension for the future, but because I was overwhelmed by all the kindness shown to me by everyone concerned. The Picards, Mother Elsa, the Sisters and, especially, my very special friends, John and Kanti. Why were they doing this? And why for me? I reasoned that it must be fate which had brought me to John Wilks and cemented a friendship which was to shape my life and last forever. I determined that I would do my best to live up to their expectations.

There was a week or so before the start of the new term at school and I busied myself helping Odile wherever I could and even standing in occasionally at the Post Office counter while Alexander went to the bank or conducted some other business in Prince Albert. Naturally, I often thought of my parents and was, in truth, a little homesick, but I knew that this was what they wanted for me. The days passed quickly and soon enough it was the morning of the first day of the new term at the Academy. Odile escorted me there and handed me over into the care of the Sisters. It all seemed very strange at first and, as I was the only student from an indigenous background, I was something of a curiosity among the other girls. One by one, during the breaks in lessons, they all seemed to come and ask me who I was and where I was from. However, there was no animosity of any kind and I quickly made friends with the other girls in my class. Some of these friendships endure to this day and I regularly exchange letters with my friends Alice, Bernadette and Christine in particular. I quickly realised that my understanding and experience of life was somewhat different from that of my new friends, and I think we learned a good deal from each other, as well as from the kindly and devoted Sisters to whom I owe so much. It was an institution unlike any other I have ever seen, where respect, kindliness towards others and proper standards of behaviour among the community were cornerstones of our education. The Sisters were not merely tutors. They were our guardians, our role models, our inspiration and, most of all, as we came to realise, our true friends. We were cosseted and cared for in a way in which, sadly, I expect few young students are today. Consequently, we loved the Academy and worked hard at our lessons. I absorbed all I could about every subject laid before us, and eagerly rushed home every afternoon to discuss what I had learned with Odile, who was always eager to listen to my ramblings.

    I made many friends at the Academy and Odile insisted that, periodically, I invite one or other of them over for tea or for a Sunday visit, where she would always prepare a wonderful meal for us and we would have a very happy time together. Alexander would often joke with us or have a story to tell and my friends always enjoyed their visits to the Post Office. When I look back on those happy days, it always brings a tear to my eye as I recall how kind the Picards were to me. They had no children of their own and saw little of their blood relatives, who were scattered from eastern Canada to France. For the time I spent with them, we were our own special family. I owe them so much.

My days were now filled with learning and enjoying life in Prince Albert. On Saturdays, I would often help out in the Post Office and would meet many interesting people from both the town and the surrounding farms. Whenever John came to town, he would allow some extra time to visit with us and would often walk with me for a while, talking quietly about all manner of things, just as we used to by the banks of the Sturgeon River. We would instantly fall into our familiar and comfortable relationship and would walk slowly through the streets, as John brought me up to date with life further north and I would tell him about the Academy and life in Prince Albert. Sometimes we would walk to the bridge and gaze down upon the North Saskatchewan River, as we discussed life and the world in general. My friends came to learn about John and the part he had played in my life and would sometimes joke about Kimi's three families as they used to refer to my situation. I didn't mind, in fact, I was very proud of my unique position in this respect and realised how truly lucky I was. At the Academy, I started to gravitate towards history and literature, although I was of course interested in all the subjects. Sister Gabrielle would sometimes stay a little later with me in the afternoon as we discussed literature, which was a passion with her. The other Sisters who taught me, Sister Sandrine, Sister Therese, Sister Cecile and Sister Nicole were all marvellous and managed to instil knowledge into us almost imperceptibly as they covered their respective subjects with typical flair and enthusiasm. My classmates similarly enjoyed our lessons and we were a happy community.

My friends at the Academy were quite a mixed bunch. There was Sarah Potter, whose parents had a farm just to the north of the town, and who had a lovely, down to earth view of everything. She had a talent for reducing everything to a simple logic which, as she described it, always made sense. She was robust and yet pretty with her fair hair and flashing brown eyes. Catherine Willis, a tall and elegant girl with a creamy complexion and hair the colour of burnished wood, was the daughter of a local lawyer and was always very precise in both her reasoning and, indeed, her general attitude towards life. Dear Alice Blake, a slightly built girl of irrepressible good humour, was always amusing us with a variety of little stories and tales, and yet, as we came to understand, she had a heart of pure gold and was a good friend to us all. Bernadette Miller, a quiet, dark haired girl always appeared very prim and proper and seemed to take a long time to make friends. Yet, when you got to know her, she was a true and loyal friend. My special friend, Christine Walter, was another fair haired girl, of mixed parentage, her mother being Danish and her father English. She had powder blue eyes, a beautiful smooth skin and was very pretty. Her father was a surveyor and they had lived in several places before coming to Prince Albert. Christine and I got along famously right from the start. I think we were both free spirits whose experience of life so far had been somewhat out of the ordinary. She also had a lively sense of humour and we would sometimes roll about laughing over some particular situation that appealed to us. I was lucky to have such friends who, together with the Sisters, made my time at the Academy very happy indeed. And, after school, I would return to the Post Office where Odile and Alexander looked after me as though I was their own daughter. My friend has a verse which sums up those innocent days.

> Friends who make our life so sweet
> Our dreams so rich, our days complete
> Are worth much more than all the gold
> In all the stories ever told
>
> They make us smile, they make us cry
> And steal our hearts as days roll by
> Into months and years, and yet
> Among the things we won't forget
>
> Are all the happy moments passed
> Within those days which could not last
> And as they fade our hearts do swell
> With love for those we loved so well

While on the subject of friendship, I should mention the relationship between Mother Elsa and John. Of course, it was his influence that secured my place at the Academy of Notre Dame, something which certainly would never have happened without him. Even on that very first day, I noticed that they were very comfortable together and seemed to understand each other very well. With the parents of the other girls, and even the other Sisters, Mother Elsa was always very curt and proper, although her kindness was never in doubt. But with John, she seemed to develop a genuine friendship. She was fond of him. And I know that he admired her tremendously. In spite of their completely different backgrounds, they seemed to find in each other a kindred spirit. During the term time, whenever John was visiting Prince Albert, he would come and collect me from school as a surprise (although I always sensed that he was coming). On such occasions, he would deliberately arrive early in order that he could sit down and have a quiet chat with Mother Elsa in her office. It became a routine, and something which I believe both of them looked forward to. Looking back, I realise now that, actually, they were alike in many ways. They were both straight and true and caring, in ways which one rarely finds in today's society. Their hearts were of a kind which knew no bounds and were open to all that could appreciate them. How lucky I was to know them both.

As I look back now on those summer days and long winter nights, I realise that I led a charmed life. Indeed, I think we all did. We were part of a fledgling province which, while there were still hard times to come, had already been transformed by the energy and spirit of a very special group of people. A spirit which was epitomised by my very dear friend and soul mate, John Wilks. By now, I was a teenager, with my own group of friends, and well past the stage of childish attachments. But my friendship with John remained firm. It was something untouched by time or circumstance. Something deep, pure and beautiful. Times were changing however, and my life was soon to take another interesting turn, once again influenced by this remarkable man.

The Formative Years

Chapter 4. A New Direction

These days, life has become increasingly complicated. Even accomplishing straightforward tasks sometimes seems to be fraught with difficulties. But back in my school days, everything was simple. We enjoyed our studies, our friendships and living in a community where fundamental values applied. The Academy of Notre Dame de Sion was a safe haven where we could submerse ourselves in our studies and have joyful discussions around what our future lives might bring. Like most of the girls, I wasn't thinking of a specific career at that stage, but simply soaking up all the knowledge I could upon every subject which appealed to me. The Sisters would occasionally speak about our vocation in life and would encourage us to think seriously about what we wanted to do once we had left their tender care. I always thought that I would like to write, but beyond that, I hadn't really formulated any specific plans. Sometimes Sister Therese would tell us about the old, established universities in Europe, and the part they had played in producing interesting people and advances in the arts and sciences. I spoke with John about the universities in England, which he knew about, although he had never actually visited any of them. He explained that it was mostly people from well established families who attended university, and not something that was open to everyone. When I told him that I would like to attend a university, he smiled and looked thoughtful for a few moments. "Maybe you shall Kimi" was all that he said, but I knew him well enough to understand that this meant he would investigate the possibility of such a course.

I hadn't thought a great deal more about it when, one summer day, we learned from the Sisters that a brand new university was to be built in Saskatchewan. Naturally, there was much talk of where it might be established, with Moose Jaw, Regina, Saskatoon, Battleford and even Prince Albert, all lobbying for the honour of hosting the university. As we learned more, slowly but slowly, I began to picture this wonderful place in my mind's eye. Somehow, I never really thought that it would come to Prince Albert. The town just didn't seem right for a university to me. I thought it would be much more likely that the university would be created in Regina or Saskatoon. Actually, I had never been to either place, but, the more I thought about it, the more I was convinced that the new university would be located in Saskatoon. Sister Theresa smiled when I suggested this. "And what makes you so sure it will be in Saskatoon Kimi?" she asked. I couldn't give a rational explanation, I just knew that it would be in Saskatoon.

The next time I saw John, I recounted all that we had heard about the forthcoming university. It was going to be the best university in Canada, I explained to him, with a proper coverage of the arts and sciences, including a special focus on practicalities such as agriculture and engineering, which would be so important for the province. I also explained to him that I would be attending the university, just as soon as it was open in Saskatoon. He smiled quietly to himself and I knew that he would do everything he could to help me realise my dream of attending the university. But it was a dream for which I had a feeling I would have to wait some considerable time.

We kept a close eye on developments with respect to the university and I often stayed a little later in the afternoons to discuss this with Sister Therese who was particularly interested. The Sisters hoped that they would get at least a few of their pupils to the university when it was opened. However, opening seemed a long way away. We heard that a board of governors had been appointed and that Walter Charles Murray, from New Brunswick, had been appointed president. There had been meetings in Regina, with various speeches and even honorary degrees awarded, but still no sign of a physical presence. The weeks and months rolled by and we learned that Murray favoured Regina as the location for the new university. He was keen that it be a single, coherent campus and not scattered here and there. Regina seemed an obvious choice. However, I remained convinced that it would be built in Saskatoon and, even Sister Therese was coming around to this point of view. She said that if I had such a strong feeling that it would be Saskatoon, then that would indeed be where it would be built. We waited to hear more and then, on April 7th 1909, there was a vote and, sure enough, Saskatoon was chosen as the preferred site. Of course, I was absolutely determined to attend and Sister Therese and myself started planning accordingly. The Sisters were, as usual, absolutely marvellous and immediately initiated correspondence with the board of governors in order to secure a few places for their own students. Christine and I redoubled our studies accordingly, both determined to attend the new university. Naturally, I spoke with John about my aspirations and he was as enthusiastic as I was, always asking how I was getting along with my studies, and what I would study when I got to Saskatoon. He shared my dream and his encouragement strengthened my resolve even more. Perhaps for the first time, I really started to think seriously about my own future in life and what I really wanted to do. And the path was opening up ahead of me.

During the school breaks, John would collect me from Prince Albert and I would usually stay with him and Kanti for one or two days before continuing the journey north to Montreal Lake. We had so many interesting discussions and, even though by this time they had their own son, Martin, I still felt very much a part of their family and we enjoyed so many happy times together. My walks by the river with John had now become something of a ritual which everyone expected, and which we savoured between us. Often, we didn't say a great deal during these walks, but there was communication of a different kind. A closeness and communion of spirit, which I now realise, is something very rare indeed. What quirk of fate had brought our lives together? Was it destiny? Was it written somewhere in the stars? Whatever it was, I was so glad of it.

When I visited my parents on the reserve during this time, I started to understand the difficulties that they faced in a different way. As a child, I hadn't really thought much about it, but now I could see things clearly. Those of my own age had become virtual prisoners, albeit within a beautiful environment. They were prisoners of a system which, while providing for their material needs, gave little inspiration or hope for the future. Dear Sarah Campbell had built up the school to a point where it was actually very good. She now had a small staff of qualified teachers and considerably better materials than when I had attended. Furthermore, the young students were all eager to learn and, indeed, the school had become a primary focus of the reserve itself. The question was, what would the young students do when they had graduated from the school? There were some jobs on the reserve, mostly administrative in either the health centre, the school or the community centre as it was now called. But these were few and, once filled, their incumbents tended to stay in their positions. For the others, there was nothing. No jobs, no inspiration, no fulfilment. This situation concerned me greatly and I wondered what could be done. I spoke with Sarah Campbell about how the young students might be encouraged to leave the reserve and continue their education out in the wider world, as I had done myself. She agreed with me and confirmed that she often encouraged them to consider such a proposition. However, to leave all that you had ever known for a life, not only among strangers, but within a subtly different culture, was a very big step, and a step which needed to be properly planned and financed. I had been lucky. I had enjoyed the friendship and guidance of John and Kanti Wilks and, through them, the Picards and others who had helped me along the way. But most of those out on the reserve did not find themselves in such a fortunate position. I felt this keenly and, later in life, would do much to raise awareness of this situation. Consequently, my visits home at this time were a mixture of joy to be with my parents again, tinged with a certain sadness as I observed the developing situation on the reserve, although, as I was later to learn, Montreal Lake was better off in this respect than many others.

Back at the Academy, we watched with interest as plans for the university developed, the campus site was chosen and, eventually, the first stone was laid. It became clear that the university would not be ready by the time that I should really be leaving the Academy. The Sisters were sympathetic to my case and agreed that I could stay on, helping to teach the younger girls as well as continuing with my own studies. This was a situation which suited me perfectly and the Picards, bless them, were happy to continue to have me live with them. Naturally, John continued his support. He never mentioned it to me and, if asked, would deny that he was doing anything in particular to help. However, I knew from Odile that he was contributing to my upkeep and, of course, there were all the books, materials and little gifts which would miraculously appear in my room after his visits. Sometimes this would make me cry, as I couldn't see how I could ever repay him for all his kindness towards me. Odile understood this and would often come and sit with me. She used to say simply that John and Kanti loved me like their own daughter and that it was perfectly natural for them to care about my future. And then she would change the subject to some light hearted discussion or little joke and we would end up laughing together. The Post Office at Prince Albert in those days was a joyous place, full of love and good humour, due in no small part, to that wonderful woman.

Eventually, after much correspondence and discussion, I was offered a place at the University of

Saskatchewan and would be among the first intake of students, just as soon as the university opened. My friend Christine, who had formally left the Academy, had also been offered a place, but we were the only two out of several who had been proposed. But of course, the university had so many applicants, from all over Saskatchewan and, indeed, further afield as students across Canada heard about this wonderful new facility. Naturally, I was overjoyed, and started to prepare for the day when I would head down to Saskatoon. A place had been secured for me in the ladies hall of residence, so I had no accommodation issues to worry about. I wrote back and forth to both John and Kanti and my parents, all of whom shared my enthusiasm, and we planned that, when the university was formally opened, John would come and take me to Saskatoon. The days passed slowly by and I couldn't wait to start this new phase of my life. Sister Therese was excited for me and reminded me often that I had the reputation and honour of The Academy of Notre Dame de Sion to uphold when I was there. I assured her that I would do my best.

Eventually, at the beginning of May 1912, the University of Saskatchewan opened its doors and I was ready to become one of the first students (actually, the buildings were formally opened a year later). As arranged, John came down to Prince Albert and met with Mother Elsa and the Sisters to thank them for all they had done for me. We then left the Academy for the last time and returned to the Post Office, where Odile had been preparing for my departure. Among many tears and fond farewells, John and I finally rolled away and headed for the road south towards Saskatoon. I felt a strange mixture of excitement and apprehension. Of course, I was excited to be going to the university. After all, that had been my dream for so long. On the other hand, I felt as though I was moving further and further away from my roots and my family. Thank goodness for John Wilks. He was the constant link which seemed to hold everything together. He was both a link to the future and to the past. He was my guiding inspiration as well as my foundation. He provided the sense of stability which I desperately needed as I ventured into an unknown world.

On the journey south, we spoke much about the university and all the wonderful things that I would learn there. All the interesting people I would meet, and how important it was to my future life. John sensed by slight nervousness and reassured me that, if for any reason it didn't work out, I simply had to write to him and he would come down and collect me, and take me home. It was a nice safety net, although I knew that I would not be needing it. We finally arrived at the campus and, after making some enquiries, made our way to the ladies hall of residence, where John helped me with my luggage, and with the formalities of registration. My new home was a nice room overlooking the courtyard in front of the building. John brought in my things and we both remarked what a beautiful room it was and how lovely the university buildings looked. I think it then quite suddenly occurred to us both that, in all likelihood, we would not be seeing one another again for quite some time. We sat silently together for a few moments, and then John announced that he really had to return. I tried to hide my emotion, but my tears started to flow of their own accord. John hugged me tightly and whispered that I must take care of myself and then hurried out of the door, down the corridor, and downstairs. I watched from the window as he drove away in his buggy and my heart felt like lead. That evening, I wandered about the campus in order to familiarise myself. The buildings were magnificent and unlike anything I had ever seen. Tall, and constructed from a wonderful red-brown granite which imbued them with an air of solidity and purpose. Slowly, I started to feel better as I realised that, here I was, at last, at the University of Saskatchewan. My dreams were all coming true.

The next morning, I was up early and, after a shower I made my way to the dining hall for breakfast. We were all a little nervous and shy but, slowly, we made our introductions and got to know each other. After breakfast, we navigated through the halls of the main building to our respective departments and found our tutors, all of whom were dressed formally in gowns and looked very proper. My primary subject areas were literature and history, although, over time, I would add various aspects of the social sciences. My literature tutor was a slim, studious looking man with round spectacles by the name of Prof. Michael Shannon. At first, he seemed a little aloof and fairly strict in his requirements of us. Over time however, I realised that he had a real passion for literature and that I could learn a great deal from him. Consequently, our tutor-student relationship developed nicely and we enjoyed many fascinating discussions about literature and poetry. He introduced me to the work of Robert Browning and John Donne, for which I shall be eternally grateful to him. My history tutor was a large gregarious man by the name of Prof. Alan Tawney. He was good humoured and was also passionate about his subject, bringing history alive in his exciting lectures, of which I attended every one. The university also had a wonderful library which grew over time and in which I could happily loose myself for many hours.

I quickly adapted to university life and loved every minute of it. There was so much around me, so much to take in and understand, and I absorbed it all like a sponge. I was so absorbed in my studies that, sometimes, there seemed little enough time to socialise, although I quickly formed a close circle of friends. My friend Christine Walter from the Academy was studying the Earth Sciences and we used to enjoy chatting about our different subjects together. Then there was Gwen Richards, a very bright girl, studying classical literature and languages, Kathleen Boult who was the beauty among us and always had a stream of admirers, and my dear friend Marcia Greg who was quiet and gentle, but very bright and seemed to pick everything up without effort. We came into contact with the male students of course and would often get together in mixed groups to chat and relax in the evenings. It was a wonderful environment, which I tried to convey in my letters home, to John and Kanti and to the Picards, with all of whom I maintained a constant flow of correspondence. However, I was conscious that I was changing. I was finding myself as an individual and was, increasingly, in control of my own destiny. I no longer needed to be helped and supported in the way that I had been previously. In short, I was slowly gaining my independence.

And yet, I was so grateful for all the help and love that I had received, both from my parents and all those wonderful people in northern Saskatchewan whose paths had intertwined with my own. Looking back on those times, I realise just how special these people were. Their origins were varied and yet they shared a common spirit of community, the strength of which is rarely found today. They had all taken their chances in a fledgling province and, through their own efforts had made it work. The only regrettable factor was the failure of the settlers and indigenous peoples to really mix and share in the prosperity of the developing province. It was a difficult situation as the cultures, while having a good deal in common, were fundamentally different.

The Cree way of life into which I was born and raised was very different from the European model. We were following traditions which had been laid down over literally thousands of years and which were still perfectly valid. We had a close affinity with nature and were able to exist in harmony with the land around us, without the need to change anything. The European approach was to transform the land to its own requirements, destroying much of what, to us, was very special, and replacing it with intensive agriculture. By the time the Cree communities realised what was going on, the die had already been set and a division created between the two cultures. Creating reserved lands where the Indians, in theory, could continue with their own way of life, was, in hindsight, a poor compromise. The Indians could not continue with their previous lifestyle because a major factor of that existence relied on the ability to roam across the land on a seasonal basis, following the available game and natural produce accordingly.

On the reserves, while they were often significant parcels of land in themselves, this simply wasn't possible in the same way. Furthermore, the provision of housing

A New Direction

and basic sustenance to the Indian bands, created a dependence upon the state which they had never experienced before, and the implications of which were perhaps not initially well understood. It was such a shame as, in fact, both cultures had much to learn from each other. From my privileged position, I could see this very clearly. Interestingly, John Wilks also understood this perfectly and tried his best to bring about a better understanding on both sides. We often discussed this issue and he was always looking for ways to bring about improvements. Indeed, he worked tirelessly on behalf of my own community up at Montreal Lake and was highly regarded and respected by all there. But that was unusual. On the reserves, there tended to be a growing mistrust of what was seen as governmental interference and a continued isolation of their own communities. Later in life, I would undertake my own research in this area.

I saw much less of John and Kanti now, and indeed, my own parents. During the summer recess I would always head north for at least a week or two and, of course, my dear friend John would transport me around wherever I wanted to go. I would take the train from Saskatoon to Prince Albert, from where John would collect me. Naturally, I would always call in at the Picards and, on John's insistence, we would also call in at the Academy of Notre Dame. I think he wanted to show the Sisters that I was progressing nicely, thanks to all their efforts. Of course, I was also delighted to meet with them again and dear Mother Elsa always received us with the utmost courtesy. Then we would head north and I would spend a few days with John and Kanti. Dear Kanti. In some ways, I think she envied my experience at the university and would ask me again and again, what I had been studying, and all about my friends. But in other ways, Kanti, perhaps more than any other Cree woman of my acquaintance, loved the land and remained in tune with nature throughout her life.

Her marriage to John was the most perfect match that I ever saw. They were almost as one person and so deeply connected that they would frequently finish sentences for each other during our conversations. Even in their letters to me, it didn't really matter who started the letter, they would both write some lines, as if in a single voice. They loved the same things and were both as honest, true and caring as it is possible to be. As I was to discover, they were also both courageous and upstanding as individuals. But my life was taking its own course now and I didn't see as much of them as I would have liked, although, whenever we did meet, we instantly fell into our old relationship and, in some ways, I felt like a little girl again. The magic never quite disappeared.

Back at the university, we continued with our studies and our academic lives. I was thinking seriously now about my future and decided that I wanted to be a journalist and, perhaps later on, an author in my own right. I was reading more and more, and developing my own views and perspectives on current affairs and life in general. Our social lives continued also and I became friendly with a young man by the name of George Radford who was also studying history, including ancient history and, his particular passion, archaeology. We were good friends and had a brief and gentle romance, although it was clear that we were not really meant for each other. However, George introduced me one day to a friend of his named Eric Anderson, who was studying engineering and with whom he often had discussions about engineering in the ancient world. Eric and I were attracted to each other right from the start. I saw in him the sort of quiet strength of character that I had seen in John Wilks. He was rather shy, yet confident in his own understanding of things and extremely well mannered. We spent an increasing amount of our spare time together and George, bless him, understood our relationship immediately and remained a good friend to us both. At the next recess, Eric introduced me to his parents. I think they were initially a little surprised that their son, who had been raised in a very well to do family, was friendly with an Indian girl. However, whatever their initial feelings were, they were absolutely delightful and welcomed me into their family circle. After a hesitant start, Eric's mother, Marie, seemed to take a shine to me and we quickly became friends. His father, Arthur, was a lawyer in Saskatoon and they lived in a large, well appointed house in the old section of the town, just the other side of the South Saskatchewan River. It was within walking distance of the university and, consequently, Eric would often take me to lunch with them at the weekends. I now had a fourth family. My friend has a verse about families.

Families are like branches bound
Together, true and strong and sound
Their constitution shall remain
Through endless trials of toil and pain

And in the family bosom beats
A heart of gold that seldom meets
A challenge that it cannot face
Or situation turned to waste

For families are the staff of life
And while our troubles may be rife
There lies a haven always near
Within that jewel we hold so dear

So never fail to judge the worth
Of all the roots that gave you birth
And in your heart for ever more
May the family be its core

It was a subject I often thought about. How families are both the inspiration and the pattern for future generations. However, the focus within families varies tremendously depending upon culture, exposure to education, tradition, external influence and a number of other factors. For some, this can become a constraint. I was so lucky in that my extended family, while from varying backgrounds and circumstances, shared a common thread of ethical values and belief. Within my Cree family, traditional values of decency and honesty were the bedrock upon which the family was founded. My exposure to European culture, mainly through John Wilks, served to reinforce and complement those ideals. Throughout my early life, I was surrounded by kindly and strong individuals who were, to coin a phrase, the salt of the Earth. They shared with me their knowledge, their experience, their hopes and their dreams. The value of their influence is beyond estimation. I considered them all as my family although, naturally, there remained a special place in my heart for my parents, whom I loved dearly. Culture aside, I realise now that there are no finer people than my mother and my father. Their quiet dignity and understanding remains a beacon in my life.

Chapter 5. The Future Unfolds

And so, my life at the University of Saskatchewan continued. I was enjoying my studies, my social life and, especially, my deepening relationship with Eric. I was already thinking that, maybe, this was the man with whom I wanted to share my life, although, at that juncture, we had not discussed any such possibility. We enjoyed many weekends at his parents house, where I got to know Marie and Arthur very well. They were a lovely family and had brought Eric up with solid, old fashioned values, which I appreciated greatly. What with this situation and my ongoing studies, which I was enjoying tremendously, the world seemed like a stable and wonderful place. And then, in late July of 1914, we heard the awful news from Europe that, following the assassination of Archduke Ferdinand in Sarajevo, a major war had broken out between the Austro-Hungarian empire and Serbia. Events escalated quickly, with Russia coming to the defence of Serbia, Germany aligning with the Austrian cause and, by association, France and Britain quickly being drawn into the conflict. Our comfortable, care-free lives suddenly took on a different complexion as we watched and waited for the news from Europe. And then, on August 5th 1914, the Governor General announced that Canada was at war with Germany and Prime Minister Robert Borden immediately offered our support to Great Britain.

When I heard that news, my heart sank and I felt cold inside. I knew straight away that, somehow, John Wilks was going to be involved in the conflict. The Canadian Minister of Militia and Defence, Mr. Sam Hughes, had been tasked by the Prime Minister to put an army together and volunteer stations were quickly established across Canada. Within the first two months alone, more than 30,000 young men had volunteered to return to Britain and fight for the allies. Eric and I discussed the situation with his parents. He was prepared to volunteer, but, after pleadings and logical arguments from both myself and his parents, he agreed that he would only go if conscripted. Fortunately, conscription in Canada didn't occur until the very last year of the war and Eric was never called upon to serve his country. However, it wasn't Eric I was worried about. I never thought that he would fight in the war. No, it was John Wilks that I was worried about. Knowing him as I did, I realised that he would feel a strong sense of duty and would want to volunteer, even though he was no longer a young man.

At the first opportunity during the recess, I travelled up to Prince Albert and met John at the station. Our very close relationship meant that he knew, that I knew, that he was considering volunteering. The moment our eyes met, my worst fears were confirmed. I read in his eyes all the reasons why he would find it imperative that he volunteer for active service in Europe. As we headed out across the bridge and onto the road north, I asked him simply, "Does Kanti know yet?" He looked at me for a moment. "She knows that I have been thinking about the situation in Europe". "But it is not your fight John, you belong here with Kanti and Martin". He looked straight ahead as if focused on some important point on the horizon and I knew that it was useless to try to dissuade him. He told me that he hadn't yet decided in any case, and then went on to explain how everything we had built up in Canada could be in jeopardy if the allies lost the war. I said that it was for younger men to volunteer and he replied that, as a craftsman, his skills might prove invaluable. When we arrived at the house and Kanti greeted me with her usual hug and smiles, I looked into her eyes and could see that she knew. Later in the evening as I helped her prepare a meal, we spoke quietly and she asked me if John would be all right in Europe. It was a terrible question to ask, but I understood why she asked it. She knew that, where John was concerned, I always had a strong intuition about things. I thought for a moment and replied that he would return safely from Europe. I felt that much, but I also knew that he would be deeply affected by his experiences there. He came into the kitchen and, knowing straight away that we had been discussing his situation, he smiled and repeated that he hadn't yet decided whether to volunteer or not. He had told Kanti that, if he did volunteer, Martin, who was now a teenager, would be able to continue with the carpentry business in his absence and that his good friends Veijo and Anja Kankkunen would be able to keep an eye on them and ensure that they had everything they needed. The pattern was set and I knew it was only a matter of time before the inevitable happened. After my visit to my parents, I stayed with John and Kanti for another couple of days and nothing at all was said about the war. Nothing needed to be said. I could read in their eyes exactly what was going on. I mentioned to Kanti that Saskatoon wasn't all that far away and that, if she ever needed anything, Eric and I could come to the house. She simply smiled gently and continued what she was doing. When John took me back to Prince Albert, he promised that he would write soon and tell me his decision. I didn't have long to wait.

Back in Saskatoon, Eric's father explained that, even if John volunteered now, it would likely be several months before he saw active service. He had been following the news closely and it seemed that volunteers were being sent to Winnipeg and Toronto for training and then over to England for more training, before finally being sent to France. Its strange, but it seems that everyone was completely shocked at John's decision to volunteer, except for myself and Kanti. We both knew that his unshakeable sense of right and wrong, mixed with an equal sense of duty, both to Canada and Britain, would make it impossible for him to sit quietly while others fought the war. He would have to be there, doing whatever he could. A week or so after his first letter, I received another letter, this time from Winnipeg. He had been enlisted as a non commissioned officer, a Corporal, and was about to begin his training. We heard news from various quarters about other Saskatchewan men volunteering. Even one or two of our tutors at the university had volunteered, and one of Eric's father's junior colleagues had also signed up. The Picards wrote and told me that many men from Prince Albert had also volunteered, and that it had had an affect upon the town. The war started to adopt a horrible and dark profile in my mind as I realised that many of these brave young men would never return home. Already, there were terrible stories in the newspapers about casualties on the fighting front, that made me feel sick inside. When I thought of that dear man, John Wilks, going into this, I shivered. I never thought that he wouldn't survive, but I was terribly worried about what horrors he might go through over there. The weeks passed and I continued to receive spasmodic letters. It seemed that they would likely remain in Canada for the winter months. At least we could rest easy for now.

And so life returned to something of an equilibrium. The news from Europe was worrying, but it all seemed a very long way away. Furthermore, Canadian troops had not yet become significantly involved in the conflict. Some were saying that it might all be over by the end of the year and that, maybe, Canadian troops would not be involved at all. It was a comforting suggestion, but I didn't believe it for a minute. I knew, in my heart, that this would be a long and terrible conflict. However, in that autumn of 1914, we were happy enough in the cosseting embrace of university life. There was always something interesting going on and we would spend our evenings and weekends among our friends, sometimes on the campus, sometimes at the homes of the students who lived in Saskatoon. I continued to enjoy my studies and I wrote frequently to Kanti, as well as keeping up the correspondence with my parents and the Picards. Kanti's letters were filled mostly with news about Martin and how he was looking after his father's carpentry business, or about visits from Veijo and Anja. Sometimes, Anja would stay for a day or two to be company for Kanti and they would enjoy their chats together. She would usually end her letters with some comments about John and wondering where he was at that moment. I could sense that she was missing him terribly and I resolved that I would visit her during the spring recess, in order to cheer her up a little.. In the meantime, we enjoyed life in Saskatoon. My friend Kathleen lived not too far from the campus and would occasionally organise Sunday lunchtime gatherings at her parents house, which became something of an institution. There was a piano in the house and Kathleen's mother was an accomplished pianist. In fact, Kathleen herself was also quite talented musically and the house would be filled with music and laughter. It was a lovely contrast to our studies and something of a release from the cares of the world.

The autumn came and went and the new year was soon upon us. Letters from John were brief and just mentioned the seemingly endless training and the fact that he was well and missing us all. I suppose I was lulled into a false sense of comfort until, in May 1915, I received a very hurried letter that his unit, the 28th Battalion were sailing for England. Eric's father maintained that it would still be some time before they saw active service. He was usually right about such things and I trusted his judgment. From now on though, it would be difficult as letters from John would become increasingly spasmodic and we never quite knew where to send our letters for him. Several weeks after his cryptic note about departure, I received another, longer letter which explained that they had sailed from Quebec on the 28th May on the S.S. Northland. The crew, he said, had been marvellous and had done their very best to look after the men on the voyage. They arrived at Plymouth on June 11th and travelled by train to London and then down to Shornecliffe in Kent, where, apparently, there was a large training complex, preparing men for the front. John's battalion were transferred to the Dibgate Camp, nearby at Sandgate. He described it as a very pleasant location, high on the cliffs overlooking the sea. Naturally, I knew that, whatever the situation, John would always portray it in a good light, so as not to worry Kanti or myself. In time, we became quite adept at reading between the lines and constructing a more realistic picture of the situation. But for now, thank God, he was not actually fighting. The worst part for us was the waiting. We never knew when another letter might arrive, or where John actually was. Of course, many others were in exactly the same position and it seemed that, whenever people got together, it was not long before they were discussing the war and the plight of their loved ones. At this juncture, such discussions were largely academic. Later on, they were often to become tragic.

Eric's parents, Arthur and Marie, were wonderful throughout this period. I had quickly become one of the family and they were always asking if I needed anything and generally doing their best to look after me. I visited Kanti as planned and spent three weeks with her in the summer, walking by the river and talking, cooking meals together in the kitchen and fondly remembering our earlier days together. Martin was looking after things very well in his father's absence and we were visited once or twice by Veijo and Anja. When Keke learned that I was at the house, he also came to visit and we had a lovely day together. It was clear that Kanti was certainly not going to be lonely. The Wilks house, as usual, was a centre for everything happening in the area, and people called by quite frequently. We had a lovely time together and I was sad to have to return to the university. But life must go on and, back in Saskatoon, things quickly returned to normal and my relationship with Eric grew deeper with every passing day. And the days passed slowly enough as 1915 progressed along its path, the news from Europe becoming ever more dreadful. We heard little from John for the next month or so until, once again, a very hastily scribbled note, this time from Folkestone, indicating that they were about to board ship for France. It was dated September 17th. I could only imagine what places like Sandgate and Folkestone were like, but such thoughts were now overtaken by the reality that John was now on his way to fight in France. It was as if a dark cloud had lodged itself in my heart. I wondered how Kanti must be feeling.

From now on, communication was erratic and John's letters varied greatly in their length and level of detail. Sometimes, they consisted of just a very few hastily scribbled lines, telling us that he was well and that conditions were generally good. At other times, he would mention the other men and describe the place where they were at that moment. He always gave the impression that everything was fine and never mentioned the loss of his comrades or the details of battle. Of course, we knew that he was hiding it from us and this, in some ways made it worse. We knew from the newspaper reports, the terrible losses being inflicted on what they called the Western Front. We also realised that this was exactly where the 28th Battalion were deployed. John and his comrades must have been going through hell, but he would never tell us. Slowly, we noticed that he began not to mention his friends. After a while, he never spoke of them, except in a remote sort of way, saying that they were all bearing up well and that they had many bright moments. The more he assured us that everything was fine, the more I worried about him. Occasionally, I would wake up in the middle of the night with a start, having been dreaming of walking by the Sturgeon River with John. It made me wonder whether something had happened to him. On such nights, I shed many tears for John Wilks. I also wondered how the wives of all those men must have felt. It wasn't long before Canadian casualties started to be posted in the newspapers, and looking down the lists became a harrowing experience as you recognised familiar names. Saskatchewan, after all, remained sparsely populated at that time and family names tended to be recognised, almost across the province. This was especially so for those in northern Saskatchewan, from where the bulk of the original 28th Battalion came. Many were to receive heartbreaking news about the plight of their loved ones. Others stopped receiving news at all, which was especially worrying. But John's letters reached us, albeit spasmodically, and we all wrote to him at the last known address, although we didn't really know if he would ever receive the letters. Usually, they caught up with him in due course, somewhere along the line.

War is such a terrible thing. Conflicts are invariably conceived and orchestrated by politicians, yet it is ordinary, decent people who pay the price. The soldiers bear the brunt of it, but it is equally hard for the families left behind. When young fathers are lost, young mothers are left to bring up their babies single handedly. For those out on the prairie, this would be especially hard and many dreams were shattered in such a manner. For some, family members and friends rallied round and helped them to carry on. For others, the dream was over. Everything they had worked so hard for now seemed as nothing, and they would pack up and leave the province altogether. Of course, it wasn't just husbands, but sons, brothers, uncles and close friends. My heart bled for them. At the university, we had many debates about the war, its causes, its likely outcome and the enormous cost in human life, which was already becoming apparent. But, in another sense, war often brings out the best in people. There were many stories of heroic action at the front and, back home, people became even more community minded and ready to help those who needed it. In north west Saskatchewan, which I considered home, this was always the case, the war simply accentuating the camaraderie among the homesteaders and other settlers. The conflict also resonated among the indigenous peoples and it was curious, and quite touching, to see many Indians volunteering for service. It wasn't their war, by any stretch of the imagination, but they were Canadians and Canada had declared war on Germany. Some of them went into the 107th, 14th and 114th Battalions, including many from the File Hills community in Saskatchewan. I was proud of them. But it was hard to understand what this war was really all about and what it was supposed to achieve. My friend captured aspects of this futility in a verse which was handed to me after the event.

What is it that we're fighting for?
Said all the men who went to war
Why should we be brought to kill
Those who never served us ill?

And both sides kept their own account
Of those who died upon the mount
And in the mud and sludge and rain
And canon's roar that masked the shame

And some returned to tell the story
But their's was not a tale of glory
And some would never speak again
But deep inside they felt the pain

And after all is said and done
And flags announce a victory won
What is there to celebrate?
The fall of those who once were great

And so we fell into a pattern of waiting for news and fearing the news we didn't want to hear. I was certain that John would return safely and reassured Kanti of this in my letters to her. But I also felt that he would be hurt in some way. In Canada, people bought Victory Bonds to help the war effort and everyone wanted to help in whatever way they could. However, there was little that we could do in a practical sense. So we waited. And waited. In the meantime, we got on with our lives and planned for the future. Encouraged by Prof. Shannon, I submitted an article about life in

Saskatchewan to a newspaper in Toronto and, to my surprise, it was accepted for publication. Thereafter, from time to time, I submitted further articles to a variety of newspapers. Some were accepted, many were not. But I was learning my craft as a future journalist. Eric was progressing very well with his studies and aimed to earn a degree in engineering. I had no doubt at all that he would achieve his objective, it was simply a matter of time. I spent more and more time with the Andersons and was effectively absorbed into their family. Eric had a brother named Peter, with whom I also got along well.

When I next had the opportunity to visit Kanti, she was very pleased to see me and we spent many hours chatting together, while Martin worked away in the workshop and tended to Bess. Occasionally, I would notice a distant and rather sad expression come over her, and I would know that she was thinking about John. At such moments, I felt anxious that my presence might have stirred up past memories, and Kanti seemed to sense this, quickly transforming here features into a smile and embarking upon some unrelated topic of conversation. Naturally, she missed John terribly, and while we would sometimes mention him in passing, it was clear that she didn't wish to discuss his situation in any detail. I understood this perfectly and so we fell into our old routine of keeping each other company as we pottered about around the house and vegetable garden. Kanti enjoyed hearing about my studies and life at the university and, of course, asking about Eric and our relationship. Veijo and Keke also visited while I was there and we had a lovely lunch together. Keke, while some years older than Martin, was a good friend to him and the two enjoyed spending time together. They were alike in many ways. Both of them gifted and yet relatively shy. Keke had become expert at managing the Kankkunen farm and Martin was displaying excellent skills at carpentry as well as taking an interest in the land around him. They both echoed their fathers to some degree, and yet were individuals in their own right. It was a fascinating thing to see.

As I travelled back to Saskatoon my mind was a jumble of thoughts and memories. I was a self assured adult now, with plans for the future. And yet the past still played an important part in my life. After all, I was a product of that past, and of all those who had taken part in it. Suddenly, I thought of Margaret Sim. I remembered how John was very fond of her, and how he was so affected by her passing. How she had been so kind to me. It reminded me that we walk on this Earth but for a short time, and that our lives are defined partly by how we react to other people and how they, in turn, see us. As the train rattled its way south from Prince Albert, I looked out from the window at the golden fields, stretching to the horizon under a powder blue sky. And then I thought of John and I knew that, at that very moment, he was also thinking of me. Our friendship could not be broken, even by war.

The Future Unfolds

Chapter 6. A New Life

Time marches on and all things must pass eventually. And so it was with the war. We waited through those agonising years for news of our loved ones. Every week, we heard of terrible losses and, every so often, someone in Saskatoon, Prince Albert, Moose Jaw or somewhere else in Saskatchewan would receive the worst news of all, as the list of good men lost grew longer. And then, in the autumn of 1918, brighter news started to appear. Bulgaria surrendered on September 29th at Saloniki, and then the Ottoman Empire followed suit on October 30th at Moudros. Austria followed on November 3rd at Padua and then, finally, Germany surrendered on November 11th at Compiegne, signing the necessary papers in a railway carriage. The war was over and everyone gave a sigh of relief. Their loved ones were safe. But for some, there was a cruel irony as many men continued to die of their wounds before ever reaching home. Of the survivors, some had suffered terrible injuries and would never be the same again. Others carried their scars inside. But all were affected in one way or another. It resonated with me that, the last soldier to die in combat on the Western Front, just as the armistice was being signed, was from John's battalion. The 28th Battalion of the 6th Brigade of the Canadian Corps.

In the coming weeks and months, returning soldiers slowly started to trickle into Canadian ports and find their way home. It was a masterly exercise of organisation as hundreds of thousands of fighting men were brought back from the battlefields of Europe to Britain, Canada and elsewhere. But it was to be quite some time before the 28th Battalion were to return. We received letters from John explaining that they had been in Germany and were now making their way back through Belgium and France. He said that there was no use in writing back to him as the letters would probably never reach him. The main point was that he was safe and well and would be coming home just as soon as he could. On June 2nd, I received a hurriedly scribbled note to say that the 28th Battalion were in Liverpool and about to board the S.S. Cedric bound for Montreal. It was dated May 19th. That would mean that they had probably already arrived and that John was on his way home. In fact, it was another five days before he reached Prince Albert and his friend Ralph Pendlebury drove him up to his beloved house by the Sturgeon River. He was home at last.

By this time, I had received my primary degree and was teaching at the university while continuing with my own studies. Consequently, it would be many weeks before I had the opportunity to travel up to Prince Albert and on to visit John and Kanti. I wrote to them of course, and included the news that Eric and I were to be married and that I hoped they would be able to attend the wedding in Saskatoon, the date of which was not yet settled. As soon as we were able, Eric borrowed a small truck and we drove up to Prince Albert, calling in at the Picards, and then on up the northern road and across on the trail to the Wilks house. Usually, John would have collected me from Prince Albert, so this was to be something of a surprise, especially as this would be the first time that they would meet Eric. We arrived at the house and Kanti was overjoyed that I had brought Eric along. I had been a little apprehensive as the Wilks household was very different from what Eric had been used to, but I needn't have worried as Eric quickly fell into the pattern of life. He was fascinated by the workshop and spent a good deal of time with Martin discussing their methods and machinery and trying his hand. The two of them got along very well together. Kanti quickly took to Eric and fussed over him, plying him with endless cups of coffee and biscuits and telling him how proud they were of me, almost as if she was my mother. It was very touching.

John was also very pleased to see us and enjoyed talking with Eric, although I noticed that he was rather quiet. When I was alone with Kanti, she told me that he was sad inside but wouldn't speak of his experiences during the war. We reasoned that it would take a little time for him to readjust back to life on the prairie, just as it would for all the returning soldiers. Kanti said that she wished he would talk to her about it and share the burden, but she understood that he didn't want to worry her. I said that I would talk to him later on as, perhaps, he might find it easier to speak with me. I also mentioned that I had seen a list of the returning soldiers, their rank and, where applicable, awards, and noticed that John had been awarded both the Military Cross and the Distinguished Conduct Medal. This was a complete surprise to Kanti as John had said nothing about this. We searched and found the medals, in their boxes, hidden at the back of the wardrobe. I explained to Kanti that the Military Cross was typically awarded for outstanding bravery as she held it gently in her hand. Tears rolled gently down her cheeks as she stood silently contemplating the medal. I placed my arm around her briefly and then left her alone with her thoughts.

Looking back, it was strange, but the very few times I ever saw Kanti cry, it was always for love of John. It seemed that there was nothing else in this world that would ever move her to tears. When I was a child, she was always kind to me and looked after me like a cross between a big sister and a mother, and of course I loved her accordingly. It was in later years that I came to understand what a wonderful person Kanti really was. John often said that his house was just a structure of wood and stone before Kanti came and turned it into a home. She had a way of putting everyone at their ease and would always share whatever they had with anyone who came to the house. And people came from every direction to the Wilks house. Indians from the north would occasionally call in, as would homesteaders from the west and south, travellers making their way up to Lac la Ronge or Montreal Lake, and various individuals from Prince Albert. Everyone knew the Wilks house and make a point of visiting if they were in the vicinity. John would make them welcome, but Kanti always made them feel at home. She retains this quality today.

I managed to tear John away from Eric and Martin and insist that we go for a walk together, just as we always used to. He was a little hesitant as he knew of course that I was going to ask him about the war, but, as I took his hand and lead him towards the river, he smiled gently and seemed pleased that we were walking together, just as we used to. We walked slowly up towards the woods as the sun glistened off the water and big, purple dragonflies darted back and forth. I pointed out places on the banks that had been our favourite spots when I was just a child, and John was thrilled that I remembered everything so clearly. Eventually, I asked him why he was not discussing his wartime experiences with Kanti and explained that this was upsetting her. "What do you want me to say Kimi?" he said, his eyes riveted on the ground, "you've already seen it all in the newspapers and probably know more about it than I do". I explained that he needed to talk about his personal experiences and let Kanti help to put those memories to rest. He stopped and turned towards me, his sad eyes looking straight into mine. For a moment, I saw everything, and realised the gravity of those awful memories. I placed my arm into his and we walked on silently.

After a while we stopped and gazed out over the bend in the river as it wound its way into the woods. Birds were twittering away in the background and the river burbling as little eddies were created around the stones along the bank. We saw some trout waving gently as they faced upstream and the current worked around them. "Kanti knows that you were injured" I said quietly. "It was nothing. A minor shrapnel blast. Many of us got caught in that way". I placed my arm around him. "We also found your medals" I continued. He breathed in deeply and said nothing. After a pause, I squeezed him and said, "If you can't talk to me, who can you talk to? There are no secrets between us". He gently placed his arm around me and looked out into the distance. "Some things are best left unsaid Kimi. What good would it do to tell you all the details?. How men fought and died?

How they suffered? It would serve no purpose". "But sharing it with us would take away some of the pain" I suggested. He took me in his arms and hugged me tightly for a moment before taking my hand and walking on. He then told me about some of the men and how he still saw their faces and heard their voices every night. He told me how they had to step over bodies in the trenches, about the stench of death, the cold and the noise. Then he said, "I'm sorry Kimi, I shouldn't have said anything. Not to you of all people, and especially not now". I hugged him and said, "but why don't you tell Kanti?". He remained silent and looked out over the river again. Naturally, I understood his point of view and how he wanted to shield Kanti from the realities of war. He agreed that, slowly, he would talk to her and perhaps tell her about some of his comrades in the battalion.

The conversation then turned to our forthcoming wedding and how happy John was for me. And that was the only time that I ever spoke to John about the war. Kanti told me later that he did try to tell her some of his experiences, although the stories never got very far. And then, one day, they were visited by Bill Christie, one of the men who had served in John's unit. He was leaving Saskatchewan and wanted to call in on John and Kanti before he left. Over lunch, he mentioned that John had saved his life and apparently became quite emotional about it, telling how John had risked his life running through enemy fire to come and rescue Bill and another injured man from a shell crater close to the enemy lines. Naturally, Kanti knew nothing about this as John would certainly never mention such things. After Bill left, she asked John about it, and, of course, he played it down and said that it was just one of those things that happened every day in the trenches. Nevertheless, we started to get a feel for John's conduct during the war and could see that he had been a hero. He joined as a corporal and came out a lieutenant, decorated for bravery and exemplary conduct under fire. We were all very proud of him, none more so than Kanti.

Back at the house, we discussed our wedding plans and how we would get everyone together down in Saskatoon. John and Kanti were most enthusiastic and started to plan the logistics of gathering everyone together. Eric explained to them that we were to be married at the recently completed St. John's church, overlooking the river in Saskatoon, describing it to them in detail and then telling them all about his parents, who Kanti was so looking forward to meeting. For a moment, I sat back and watched quietly as they joyously discussed the forthcoming event. Was this really all happening to me? It seemed like yesterday that I was a young girl playing by the river and helping John in his workshop, before Kanti would call us inside for some snack or other which she had prepared. I looked at those dear faces, all of whom I loved so well, and realised, once again, how truly lucky I was. Eric and I stayed for a couple of days before returning to Saskatoon. Kanti wanted us to stay longer, but there was so much to arrange. I was pleased that they had all got along so well. Eric had shown John the truck and they had gone for a little ride together. I could see that John was becoming greatly interested in motorised transport. Eric and Martin had spent some time in the workshop where Eric had tried his hand at making a few pieces. And, of course, Kanti and I had managed to spend some time chatting and, to my relief, she was very taken with Eric and assured me that we would be very happy together. Kanti was very wise when it came to human relationships and her opinion meant a great deal to me. She was also very enthusiastic about the wedding and clearly looking forward to it. It was a lovely visit.

In Saskatoon, together with Eric's parents, we started to plan the wedding properly, booking the church and making accommodation arrangements for all who would attend from further north. It was a magical time for me. A combination of happy organisation and looking forward to our future life together as man and wife. My friend quietly passed to me a little verse which seemed to capture the moment.

> A man may wander through his days
> Forever searching to find ways
> To bring a meaning to his life
> Until the day he takes a wife
>
> The meaning then comes from afar
> Shining like the northern star
> And all the heavens there above
> Gaze down upon their tender love
>
> A man and woman thus entwined
> Savour all the joy they find
> Together through the days they live
> And all the love their hearts do give
>
> And future generations learn
> So long as worlds may ever turn
> There's nothing sweeter we shall see
> Than man and wife in harmony

So the wedding was planned and Eric and I, while still involved with the university, were planning our new life. Eric had been speaking with various organisations and it looked as though he would have more than one offer of employment. However, it also looked as though any such offer was unlikely to be from within Saskatchewan, so we were preparing ourselves for the necessity of moving. However, first there was the wedding and, soon enough, the day before the service arrived and with it, all of our friends from Prince Albert and the north, including my parents, Etchemin, my special friend Sooleawa, the Picards and of course John and Kanti. We had arranged lodgings for them at Mrs Talbot's boarding house on 20th Street where, later that day, they were to meet Eric's parents, Arthur and Marie, and go out to dinner with them. That evening, Eric and Peter celebrated with their friends, and I celebrated quietly with my friends from the university and Sooleawa, whom they were all interested to meet.

The next day, I met with Kanti, Odile and Sooleawa at the boarding house in order to dress and prepare for the wedding, while the men went for a walk after breakfast. Arthur had kindly organised some cars to pick us up and take us to the church which, actually, was only a short way from 20th Street. As I walked down the aisle with my father, the congregation turned to watch and, in the second row from the front, stood John and Kanti. My step slowed, very slightly as I caught John's gaze. Our eyes were locked together for a moment, just as the first time I ever saw him. He smiled and gave a very gentle nod of his head, and I walked on, my heart beating quickly under my dress. It was as if my entire childhood and upbringing had all taken place, just minutes before and, all of a sudden, here I was, about to marry the man I would spend the rest of my life with. The Rector, Mr. Earnest Smith, conducted the service and it all flashed by so quickly that I can remember little of it until Eric spoke the woods "I do". We were soon in the little alcove, signing the marriage certificate, and then outside in the sunshine. One of Arthur's professional colleagues was an enthusiast photographer who had agreed to take some photographs for us, and so we posed by the church while he adjusted his camera and made various plates of the occasion. As we rode in the cars back to the Anderson house, I looked at Eric and gave a deep sigh of relief. After so much planning, it had all been over so quickly and now we were man and wife. Back at the house, Eric's parents had arranged a reception lunch which we all enjoyed, before Eric and I had to change as we were leaving that same afternoon for Regina, where we would spend a week together on our honeymoon, a present from Arthur and Marie.

The wedding was, naturally, one of the most important events in my life and a harbinger of change. Shortly after we returned to the university, Eric received an offer from Canadian Pacific, which he accepted. It would mean us moving straight away to Montreal as Eric would be based in the Engineering Office, 401, at Windsor Station. I wrote to my parents, the Picards and the Wilks, explaining that they would see rather less of us now, but hoping that we would soon be able to welcome them to come and stay with us in Montreal for a few days, once we had become settled. A week or so later, after settling all our affairs at the university, we said goodbye to Arthur and Marie at the station and started the long journey East. As the train rattled along, mile after mile, I had a mixture of feelings. Naturally, I was excited and pleased to be going to Montreal with my new husband, yet, at the same time, I was sad to be leaving Saskatchewan and all the dear people that had been so much a part of my life up until that time. It was hard to remain dry eyed and Eric, sensing my feelings, placed his arm around me and promised that we would, from time to time, come back out to Saskatoon.

Canadian Pacific had kindly located an apartment for us, not far from Windsor Station and we quickly settled down to a very different life. Eric was working hard at his job and I started contacting the local newspapers and magazines, offering my services as a journalist. I managed to get one or two commissions with special interest magazines and, importantly, had articles published in both the Montreal Gazette and the Montreal Star newspapers. The work was spasmodic and developed slowly over time, but it didn't really matter as Eric was earning a good salary and we had everything we wanted in Montreal. I wrote regularly to my family and friends in Saskatchewan and, to be honest, I missed them all terribly in those first few months, none more so than John and Kanti. I fully realised that without their help, love and guidance, I would probably be back on the reserve up at Montreal Lake. I thought of them every day, and prayed that they would remain safe and happy. But life must move on, and we must follow our dreams to wherever they lead. Mine had lead me to Montreal, to be with the man I loved and to pursue my career as a journalist.

A New Life

Chapter 7. Changing Times

And so our life settled into a comfortable routine as Eric prospered in his job and I became increasingly established as a journalist. I maintained a regular correspondence with our friends in Saskatchewan and was pleased to observe that things seemed to be going well for them also. John had bought a truck and found a new line of business in building light truck bodies to complement his furniture business, which was also doing well. At around the time of our marriage, John had lost his beloved horse Bess. She had been so much a part of his life on the prairie and, indeed, of my own. I had many fond memories of riding with John on his box cart and later in his buggy, with Bess happily trotting along. Kanti told me that he was broken hearted when she died. It was a relief therefore to hear that he had discovered a new interest and was keeping very busy. We also heard that John had finally persuaded Martin to attend the university. It was a struggle as Martin was never happier than when organising the workshop and helping his father to fulfil their orders, but John wanted to provide better opportunities for him, just as he had done for me. Kanti was also pleased that Martin was going to study at the university, as she knew that he was capable of better things.

Elsewhere on the prairie, their neighbours were starting to prosper on the farms. Many of them were at the point now where they had broken the land and were enjoying regular crop yields, mostly of wheat, as this is what the market wanted. They were also becoming much better organised with respect to distribution. A farmers union had been created and a wheat pool formed in order to better serve the market. The railways were also opening up the province, making it easier for farmers to transport the grain. John wrote that grain elevators were springing up all over the province, like giant statues on the horizon. He had continued with his arrangement with the Johanssens, who farmed part of his land and split the profits with him, but John had realised early on that he was not really cut out for farming. However, it was typical of him that he would often go and help his friend Veijo when the crop needed to be got in. In general, the next few years were good to the homesteaders in Saskatchewan. All of their hard work seemed to be slowly paying off and they were producing an enormous amount of wheat which, via the Winnipeg Grain Exchange, was not only helping to feed Canada, but was being exported to America, Britain and elsewhere. Saskatchewan had truly become the wheat-bowl of Canada, just as the government had intended when first drawing up the Homestead Act.

But then things started to go wrong and, for me, it meant much heartbreak as I watched from afar the changing fortunes of those I had left behind. In 1926, amid a buoyant local economy the wheat pool bought the company that owned the grain elevators and strengthened their position accordingly. It seemed that they could do no wrong as healthy crops continued to arrive. Indeed, 1928 was a bumper year with record yields and, for the first time, there was a situation of supply exceeding demand. The prices on the Winnipeg Grain Exchange were dipping and the farmers were not at all happy with the situation. They saw the grain exchange at Winnipeg as middle men seeking to profit by their hard work, without taking any of the risk. Consequently, they started to hold back supplies in an attempt to push the prices back up to where they thought they should be. However, they perhaps hadn't appreciated that some of the export markets that they had been supplying through Winnipeg, were now growing more wheat themselves and some, like the United States, put up effective barriers against imported Canadian wheat. The farmers had their elevators full, but no-one was buying, at least not at the prices they wanted to achieve. As I read the papers, I could see that things wrangled back and forth a little here and there, but in general terms, little progress was being made. It was a worrying time for the farmers who had pinned all their hopes, indeed, their very existence, on growing wheat. And then, in May 1929, the price on the Winnipeg Grain Exchange crashed to an all time low. The farmers found themselves in an impossible position. They had plenty of grain, but no market for it at anything like sensible or sustainable prices. They did what they could and, some at least, diversified into other crops, but wheat was the main produce of Saskatchewan and it was wheat that everyone depended upon.

The following months brought a great deal of discussion, but little change for the farmers. It all seemed so unfair after all the effort they had made. Then, in October of that same year came the stock market crash in America, the shock waves of which reverberated around the world. Everyone was affected in one way or another, but for Saskatchewan, it was a disaster. I watched the newspapers with horror as the depression bit hard in my home province. And then, things got worse. In 1931 there was a severe drought and many farmers started to give up the land and homes that they had loved and sweated over and leave the province completely. The next few years saw an exodus of disillusioned and broken hearted families from the province. Those who stayed, and thought that things couldn't possibly get any worse, found that things could, and did, get worse. There were serious outbreaks of flu, dust storms, more drought and record temperatures which scorched and bleached the land dry. Many who had been just hanging on, now found themselves destitute and with nowhere to turn.

Elsewhere in Canada, their plight was realised and, thank goodness, efforts were quickly made to send relief and food parcels to Saskatchewan. We heard awful stories of people dying out on the farms from a combination of illness and starvation. Animals were starving too and the situation had descended into something quite dreadful. Naturally, I was extremely worried about John and Kanti, their neighbours and, of course, my parents and their friends up on the reserve. Ironically, they seemed to fare better on the more northerly reserves and my parents wrote that they were quite well and had everything they needed. John wrote to say that he and his friend Veijo were pooling their resources and skills and that, overall, they were not doing too badly. He at least had plentiful supplies of fresh water and timber, and Veijo and Keke had had the foresight to maintain a small dairy herd. They were confident that they would be able to sustain the depression. I offered to send John some money to help out during the worst of it but, of course, he would not hear of it and said that he would send it straight back if I did. Still, I worried about them all terribly.

Just before these depression years, I had given birth to my two beautiful daughters, Merit in 1923 and Sarah in 1928. At the time, the world looked like a bright and happy place, but now, things were indeed looking rather bleak. As a family, we were faring quite well, as Eric was enjoying a good salary and I complemented this with my journalistic work. Eric remained very positive and assured me that the depression would pass and that everything would be buoyant again, even in Saskatchewan. We visited the Andersons in Saskatoon a couple of times and managed to meet with John and Kanti and the Picards in Prince Albert, but these days we were seeing very little of them. I kept inviting them to come and stay with us in Montreal for a while, but it was a very long journey and, although Kanti always said that they would come one day, I think I knew in my heart that they probably never would do so. They loved their house by the river too much to leave it for any appreciable time and, of course, Martin was not at home now. The Picards were thinking of retiring and really just wanted to settle quietly in Prince Albert. Our live's paths had diverged and were headed now in different directions. I was rather sad about this. Eric and I were successful and had everything we needed, but I still missed the Sturgeon River, the woodlands and those big, powder blue skies. They were in my blood.

My saviour were the stories that I would tell to my daughters as they were growing. Stories about my own childhood and how wonderful it was to play by the river and watch the stars in the night sky. Stories about how I would make friends with the animals and talk with them about so many things. Stories about the day I met my uncle John and how he saved my life. Stories about my mother and father, my grandparents and life in our summer and winter camps. Stories about long summer days and gathering wood for the fire on winter nights. In stories, we relive our dreams and find our true selves. My friend told me a little verse about stories.

> Stories run across all time
> Wondrous tales of every kind
> Some are sad and make us weep
> Some are treasures for to keep
>
> Some remind us of the past
> And times we knew would never last
> Some will strike us to the core
> And live with us forever more
>
> So never under estimate
> The worth of tales we do relate
> To shape our lives and steer us true
> With warmth and love in all we do
>
> And so my friends before I go
> Come fortune high or fortune low
> I shall leave you one last story
> Of hope and love in all its glory

My daughters loved my stories when they were small and would often ask to hear a favourite one again and again. They liked to hear about the golden fields and the skies so big that you could see them stretching for miles and miles into the distance. The lakes with a surface like glass which, occasionally would be broken when a trout jumped up to catch a fly. The woods with all their mystery and the trails which ran through them like the veins on a leaf. The eagles that flew overhead and the wolves that called at night. The elk and moose that wandered quietly through the trees like passing shadows. The stars that shone so brightly upon a velvet sky and the big prairie moon as it sailed down graciously to greet us. They had so many questions about everything, as all children do. But especially about my dear uncle John and his beautiful wife Kanti. I think they sensed intuitively the huge influence that John had had upon my life. No doubt they had a mental picture of the two of them in their house by the river, as I had described it so many times. They wanted to hear about how lovely Kanti was with her long black hair and graceful countenance. And most of all, I had to repeat countless times the story of my first meeting with John, when I was a mere bundle carried into his cabin close to death. They would listen in wide eyed silence as I recounted these tales.

So my life had moved on. I was a wife, a mother and a working journalist. I wrote about nature and the need for us to protect it. I wrote about the history of our land and how it had developed. I wrote about the plight of the Indians living on isolated reserves. And I wrote about the future for our children and their children. At the same time, I continued to read everything I could. I revelled in Dickens and was soothed by John Donne and

Robert Browning. I also read the news from the provinces and, while the life force seemed to be slowly moving back into Saskatchewan, there remained problems and more bad luck. In 1938, they were hit with an epidemic of horse encephalitis which swept through the province and killed many thousands of animals. This was at a time when temperatures were reaching all time highs and farming remained a risky business. Furthermore, the horse was still relied upon for many duties. It was yet another paralysing blow. And then of course the second war broke out. In some ways, this may yet prove to be an opportunity to rejuvenate industry and help to get Saskatchewan back on its feet. But for many, it will be too late.

It was just a few months ago that Kanti wrote and told me that John's special friend Veijo Kankkunen had passed away and how deeply it had affected him. It affected me too. Perhaps for the first time, I was reminded of our own mortality and that we would be dancing on this Earth but for a short time. We pass through life as though passing briefly by a window onto history. Our silhouettes, no matter how tall, all pass by the window and move on. I realised with a start, that many of those I loved dearly would not be with us for too much longer. I tried to put such thoughts out of my mind and concentrate on the moment at hand, but, deep inside, a seed of awareness had been sown. It was only a matter of time before more bad news would come and, on that fateful day described at the start of this book, I knew in my heart that my most special and dear friend was leaving us. The confirmation of the fact was not really a surprise, but it still made me freeze inside. John had gone and I would never see that kindly face again.

The face that I had known so well, and through so much of my early life. And yet, I still find myself talking to him when I am alone with my thoughts and feel, sometimes, that he is walking beside me, as he did so often on the banks of that beautiful river. When I was in the house, speaking with Kanti on the evening of the funeral, she suddenly took me by the hand and lead me outside. It was a clear night and the stars shone brightly. Kanti then pointed to one that shone more brightly than any other, and which seemed to be twinkling as if speaking to us, and said, "That is our star. It has watched over us through all these years" She then squeezed my hand gently. "John is waiting there now. Waiting for me to join him. One day soon, we shall be together again".

Changing Times

Chapter 8. Reflections

I tried to persuade Kanti to come and live with us in Montreal, so that we could look after her. She was more than welcome and it would have given me great pleasure to have her there with us. But she wouldn't hear of it. "No Kimi" she said emphatically, "This is John's house and I shall never leave it. It is where I belong. It is where all our happy days have been". Of course, I understood this perfectly and admired her all the more for it. Kanti's strength and devotion was of a kind rarely found in the modern world. I wondered what would happen to the house when Kanti also left us. Martin no longer lived there and, if the land was sold, it would be hard to imagine anyone choosing to live in the house as it was. They would no doubt think that it would need completely renovating, even if it were to be used purely as a summer house. This played on my mind as I couldn't bear to think of that wonderful home falling into neglect, as other homestead properties had done. It had been the centre of so much activity. So much happiness and love. But the world has changed, and people have changed along with it.

The homesteaders and settlers that came to Saskatchewan at the same time as John Wilks, were a special breed. They were adventurous, courageous and had a view of the world based upon solid values of integrity. John and his friends, Veijo Kankkunen, Erkki

Haajanen, Robert Turner and others were all men upon whom you could rely absolutely. Together, they forged a community spirit which simply doesn't exist today. Their readiness to share and help each other, without thought of reward or obligation was as natural as saying hello. It was the same quality which endeared John to the Indian community, with whom he enjoyed a special relationship which, actually, was quite unusual, even then. This sense of community manifested itself in many ways. When a school house was needed at the Sturgeon River junction, the men got together and built it. When any task presented itself that was greater than one man could easily manage, the others would appear as if from nowhere and help, just as happened when John was building his own house. If anyone was travelling to town, they would let their neighbours know and ask if there was anything they could pick up for them.

The women shared their talents in making clothes and items for the houses and children routinely helped out on the farm when they were not at school. John's unselfish contribution of his time and labours also made a significant difference up at Montreal Lake, where he pushed forward the construction of the school, improvements to the main lodge and many other things. And the Wilks house was a magnet for anyone travelling in the area. There was always someone or other stopping by and everyone seemed to know John and Kanti. I loved being there by the river, with the old stables shack and workshop sitting next to the rough, but beautiful stone house. There was a tangible atmosphere of goodwill and happiness which seemed to ooze from every stone and rafter. Of course, that was as much a product of John and Kanti's personalities as the raw materials, but the setting was beautiful as well, with the woodlands nestling to the north and the prairie stretching out to the west and south. And in the background, the constant burbling of the Sturgeon River, as if gently speaking to us of all the wondrous things it had seen. For a child, this was paradise. Perhaps this is why I am so concerned for its future.

My parents used to tell me about a beautiful lake, somewhere to the east of our camp, where the hearts of animals hunted for food would be placed in the woods overlooking the lake, in order that their spirits may live happily. Eventually, I persuaded them to take me there as a special treat, and I found it a mesmerising haven of peace and tranquillity. Hanging Hearts lake, as it is known, is one of the most beautiful locations in the area. Beavers swim in the lake in the early mornings and evenings, squirrels dart about through the trees, and various animals roam through the woods which, for me makes it especially interesting, as I have always had a rapport with animals.

Interestingly, so did John Wilks. He seemed to have a way of putting animals at their ease, and I noticed this on many occasions. Sometimes, when we were walking through the woods, we would come across an elk which, ordinarily, would run away. But with John, it would typically just walk a few paces and then turn and watch him as he gently spoke to it. Animals were never frightened of him. They seemed to immediately sense that he was a friend and would never hurt them. His relationship with Bess, his horse, was also very special. At first, I found it a little amusing that he would often talk to her as we wobbled our way down the trail in his box-cart or buggy. And she would respond. Sometimes by waggling her ears or, occasionally, by giving a little whinny and nodding her head. She had been his first, and constant companion since arriving in Saskatchewan and they were evidently very close friends. But John loved all animals and always tried to look after those who came near the house. There were always birds flying around the house and stables and sometimes an elk or moose would linger close for a while. At night, we would often hear wolves in the forest, but John never minded them and always regarded them as friends. In this respect, he was quite Indian-like in his attitudes to the natural world. When I was a child, we would have endless discussions about animals, insects and the fish in the river and nearby lakes. I would often have my own pet names for them and would concoct stories which, to me, reflected their various characters. John would listen patiently if I had a story to tell and would always encourage me in this activity. I had many stories about animals. And my friend had a verse for animals.

Animals in their kingdom fair
Roamed the hills and valleys where
Life's abundance met their needs
And yet provided future seeds

A balance struck was thus maintained
With little lost and little gained
Until the day that man appeared
With mechanisms to be feared

But animals are just like man
They feel and love and understand
And if we drive them from this place
We'll lose their pure and noble grace

And we shall be the losers fair
Amid the barren landscapes where
The animals no longer roam
Across the lands that once were home

It seems strange to think that, amid the neat and tidy streets of Montreal where I now live, most of our neighbours were born and raised in the city. While they had certain benefits with respect to schools, health care and the ready availability of provisions, they never experienced the magic of living close to the land. The backdrop of forests, lakes and plains made it seem as though you were like living within a beautiful landscape painting. The sounds ensured that you were surrounded by music, and the scents of the forest were like perfume. And all of these things seemed to speak directly to you.

The burbling river told a story of all the places it had been through many thousands of years. The breeze in the treetops whispered a reassuring message whenever you were walking beneath, and every tree along the way had its own story to tell. Sometimes, you would come across waterlogged sections after the heavy rains, and there would always be n abundance of life examining them, or coming to drink from them. The ever present dragonflies would dance over the water and, upon noticing you, would come and flutter right in front of your face, as though welcoming you to their home. The squirrels would be chirping and chattering, running up the bark of a nearby tree and along a branch from where they could better observe you as you walked by. And you walked on a soft, deep carpet of mosses and leaves which caressed every footstep. Everywhere was teeming with life and blazing colour.

In the wintertime, the land was transformed into a fairy tale, blanketed in white and sculpted into the most amazing shapes. It was cold, but extraordinarily beautiful. In comparison, the city is drab and colourless. There is noise, but no music. There is sculpture but no beauty. The pavements are hard and unyielding. And there is little natural life, except humans of course. Consequently, I feel rather sorry for my city friends who have never known the magic of living out on the prairie. And it isn't just the beauty of the countryside that they miss. The way of life and the attitudes of those who were living that life were completely different. No matter how hard they were working, people had time for each other. They would talk to each other and care for each other in a way that simply doesn't happen in the metropolis.

The Homesteaders - Reflections

Many such thoughts occur to me these days. Life is a fast moving kaleidoscope of different ambitions, relationships and experiences. Some of us are successful in our aspirations, some are less so, but it is our understanding and appreciation of the world, and of humanity, which tends to shape us as individuals. An essential part of this is a closeness with the natural world which, I believe, is fundamental to this broader understanding. Those who live and work on the land tend to appreciate this fact. Those who have never done so are at something of a disadvantage in this respect. Men like John Wilks, Veijo Kankkunen and the other homesteaders had this understanding and it was reflected in their own characters. Their love of the land and everything in the natural world influenced their view of humanity and the way they interacted with each other, as well as with strangers. Folk who are city born and raised tend to react in a completely different way. But of course, the homesteaders and their way of life represent a period in time which is in the process of passing. After the end of this war, I don't suppose that things will ever be the same again in Saskatchewan. Many will see this as a good thing, as the situation will undoubtedly become more stable and with a firmer industrial base. But those, like myself, who remember the old days will miss the simple, but genuine sense of community that prevailed, as well as the characters involved.

So now my thoughts go back to the funeral with which I started this narrative. As we buried my dear friend Mr. John Wilks, we buried a way of life which shall not return. As I stood by his grave side, it suddenly occurred to me that I was a middle aged woman now, with children of my own, and those that I had always thought of as young and active, were now old and tired. Veijo Kankkunen had already passed on. And now John Wilks. It wouldn't be long before their widows joined them and their neighbours as well. And then, what would become of this precious land?. I had seen so much in my lifetime. From being raised in a conventional Cree community, with its winter and summer camps, moving to a reservation, moving again to attend school in Prince Albert, on to the university at Saskatoon, and then, finally, to start my new adult life in Montreal. Throughout this time, I came to meet and admire several people who punctuated each phase of my journey. But none more so than John Wilks. He was an uncomplicated individual with iron strong principles and a heart as big as a house. He did not enjoy the benefit of a proper, formal education, yet he instinctively understood more than many who did have that privilege. Whenever I had a question about something, John would always know the answer, and his advice was always sound. He was also a craftsman of particular distinction and, as we came to discover, a brave and honourable man in times of conflict. I shall never quite know why he befriended me in the way that he did, nor shall I cease to wonder at the strength of the bond between us. There are no words to describe how I shall miss him.

At several places within this narrative, I have shared with you a small selection of verses, from a larger collection, written by a friend of mine. These were handed to me, on odd scraps of paper and torn cardboard, quietly and discretely without saying a word and knowing that I, in turn, would never discuss them. Today, I have them all in an old battered biscuit tin which once belonged to my mother, and which I now keep safely in my bedroom. It is my most treasured possession. My daughters refer to it simply as mum's tin, and tease me about it sometimes, as they wonder how a tin full of odd scraps of yellowing paper could possibly be so precious. Nevertheless, I have left them firm instructions that, when I die, my tin is to be placed in my casket and buried with me. You may be wondering what sort of a person would write little verses and pass them to me over a period of many years, from when I was a child, to after I was married, and who exactly this friend was. I shall tell you now. His name was John Wilks. And may his soul be at peace forever more.

Reflections

Chapter 9. Epilogue

I fist started writing this narrative a little over two months ago. Since that time, I have been keeping in touch with Kanti by letter and regularly telephoning the Picards in Prince Albert for news. Martin has also written once or twice and Keke's wife Lillian has been keeping in touch by telephone from their farm, which Keke still maintains. Throughout this time, I have thought much about John and Kanti Wilks and the impression they have made upon my life, although, in addition to writing this narrative, I have also had my own work to attend to, as well as looking after my family. Consequently, it has been an especially busy time.

This morning, I awoke with a start at around five thirty and I knew immediately what was wrong. I stayed at home, just waiting for the telephone call which I knew would come. It was Lillian who called me, just after lunch time. "I'm so sorry to have to tell you Kimi..." she began, and the tears started to roll down my face as she gave me the news that Kanti had passed away. I already knew it of course, it was just the confirmation of the fact which hurt so much. She hadn't been ill and appeared, outwardly at least, to be in very good spirits. It seems that she had cleaned and tidied the house, placing everything very precisely, just as it was when John was there, and then laid down to sleep for the last time on this Earth. I always knew that she would not last for long without her beloved husband. The two of them were so close that life apart from one another held little meaning.

Kanti's situation reminded me of a story that I had heard and subsequently liked to tell when I was a child. It was about an Indian princess who was well loved by everybody in the camp and had spent her life caring for others, even though her own heart had been broken. One day, the elders noticed a beautiful white eagle, which circled and came very gently to rest on the roof of her cabin. The elders knew what that meant and settled down to watch the Eagle. It stayed for some time and then slowly spread its wings and, letting out a joyous cry, it flew away, far into the distance above the forest, eventually disappearing over the horizon. The elders knew that the eagle carried the spirit of the princess with him. When they looked into her cabin, everything inside was beautifully arranged and she was lying peacefully on her bed, her spirit departed. I had a name for the eagle. I used to call him Keme. I like to think that Keme the eagle came and settled on the roof of the Wilks house, and then carried Kanti's spirit off to be with John once again, in some magical and beautiful place where they would never again be parted. Kanti had told me, at John's funeral, that they would be together again soon. I do so hope that they are.

So now I have to plan another journey back to Saskatchewan. It is a journey that I hardly relish, and yet one that I must make in order to say goodbye, for the last time, to someone I loved dearly and who had given me so much love when I was a child and, indeed, in later years. But, with Kanti's passing, I shall also be saying goodbye to a time which shall never be repeated and which was so much a part of my early life. It beings an even stronger meaning to this narrative and renders it all the more poignant as we pursue our modern lives. John and Kanti's story should never be forgotten as they, more than anyone I knew, epitomised the spirit of those special times and the coming together of two quite different cultures in a way that I always knew was possible. John had often told me about the importance of having an open heart and keeping it free of the chains of race, religion or politics. His own example was exemplary in this respect. John was an Englishman by birth and yet, with the exception of the Turners who were briefly his neighbours to the south, most of his friends were from other cultures. His immediate neighbours were mostly Scandinavian. In Prince Albert, his good friends the Picard's were French, as were the Sisters at the Academy of Notre Dame de Sion with whom he got along so well. To the north, his friends were exclusively Cree, with whom he developed a special and enduring friendship. To all of these people, he was exactly the same John Wilks, with his strong sense of integrity and care for those around him. His love for, and marriage to, Kanti, who was a full blood Cree, was as natural as the flowing waters of the Sturgeon River. They were meant for each other. More so than any couple that I have ever seen.

John and Kanti lead a relatively simple life. They had little in a material sense and were not destined to achieve any particular notoriety or distinction in their time. Yet, in other ways, they were wealthy beyond measure. They drew from a well of kindness and love which knew no boundaries, and they were surrounded by beauty of the most extraordinary kind. Furthermore, they touched the lives of so many people who, for whatever reason, had passed by that bend in the river and headed north, or indeed, had wandered south from the forests above. They epitomised the quiet courage and decency of which humans are capable, and yet so often seem to forget in their rush to fulfil their particular, and often selfish, ambitions. They also reflected a time which passed fleetingly as one era transformed into another. It was a time where solid, some would say old fashioned, values of decency and honest hard work were maintained. Where friendship and sharing meant more than accumulating wealth. Where the sense of community and togetherness was tangible.

The Great War tested these values in the men that left their golden fields of Saskatchewan to go and fight on the Western Front. It was a test which they passed with honour. Those who returned to pick up the thread were soon hit by further challenges, culminating in the depression and a terrible time for those living out on the prairie where life, at the best of times, was hard enough. But men of the calibre of John Wilks came through all of this and remained true to their values and code of conduct. John told me once about the ancient Egyptians and how they believed that, when you died, you attended a weighing of the heart ceremony, where your heart was weighed against a feather which represented your words and the testimony of those you had known in life. If it balanced, you were admitted to the court of Osiris and Isis, where you would live happily forever more. If it didn't balance, your heart would be discarded and you would be condemned to walk in the underworld for eternity. I remembered the story vividly, especially as, according to John, the ceremony was overseen by Anubis, the jackal. We both agreed that Anubis lived on in the timber wolves who roamed the forest and for whom, both John and I, had the utmost respect. It was a lovely story. In any event, I had no doubt at all that, if John and Kanti had lived in ancient Egypt, their hearts would have balanced beautifully.

Today, we are developing rather different yardsticks, based upon what we see as achievement and success. For many, this equates simply to material gain and the acknowledgement of our peers in what ever particular field of endeavour we engage. But there is a distinction between success in the material sense and success as a human being, although the two are not mutually exclusive. The ancient Egyptians evidently understood this. The success of John Wilks was not a material success, but one firmly aligned with his inherent humanity. A success not celebrated or acknowledged by a wide professional circle, but one deeply appreciated by those who knew him. It was a success which others would do well to emulate. Perhaps it was partly a product of that fleeting era that I mentioned previously. If so, then all the more reason why we should never forget the story of the homesteaders and the spirit which moved them to risk everything for a new life on the prairie. It's hard to imagine people doing this today.

In future times, people will look back on the history of Saskatchewan and they will note important milestones of those times, such as the treaties made with the Indians in the latter part of the nineteenth century, the provision of the Homestead Act and the influx of settlers and, of course, the depression years of the nineteen thirties. They will note the economic and infrastructural development of the province throughout these times, but what will they really know of the people who shaped these developments and the environment they found themselves in? Will they ever understand the thrill of seeing the early morning mist in the forest, the smell of the earth, those huge skies and the canopy of jewel like stars at night, the joy of riding in a squeaking and joggling box cart in the summer sunshine, the smell and taste of coffee heated over an open fire, warm bannock bread and herbs, the interaction with nature and an amazing variety of creatures large and small, but most of all, the warmth, laughter and companionship of so many wonderful and diverse people, united in a common cause? I suspect not. And yet, it is these things which, more than anything else, really define the spirit of those days. I was lucky. I had the opportunity to experience it at first hand. To revel in the caring embrace of a community unlike any other. A community fostered by a unique spirit, woven from the hearts of people who were culturally distinct, and yet shared common values of humanity. It is a time already forgotten by many, except perhaps those, like myself, who lived through it and understood how fast things were changing, both for the indigenous peoples and the settlers. For me personally, when they lay Kanti to rest and seal her grave, they will also be sealing those times forever.

I shall never forget. But after my generation has gone, who will remember, really remember, what made those times so special? Perhaps you are reading these few lines in a completely different time and place, long after I have gone. In which case, I hope that the story of John and Kanti Wilks, the other homesteaders and my own forefathers will strike a chord in your heart and cause you to consider afresh that which is really valuable in this life and that which is superficial. Perhaps you will come to look at the natural world and its many creations through different eyes. Perhaps you will come to cherish the wonder and warmth of true human relationships. Perhaps you might even be moved to create your own little community, founded on kindness, just as the Wilks had done, from their little house by the side of the Sturgeon River. In so doing, you would be keeping this story alive. It is, after all, a story which surely deserves to live on. But now, I must lay down my pen and make arrangements to visit, once more, that beautiful land in which I was raised. Saskatchewan. I will share with you, before I go, a last verse from my very dear friend who loved this land so much.

Epilogue

There is a land where fields of gold
Hide many dreams and stories told
Throughout the ages man to child
Of rivers deep and forests wild

And in this land there beats a heart
It's presence felt in every part
Across the plains of beauty fair
And in the forest's still night air

For this is not just any land
Sculptured by some unseen hand
This is where our dreams were won
'Neath rain and snow and burning sun

And how we've come to love the sight
Of prairie moons and stars so bright
But spare a thought for those that lay
Beneath the soil this very day

Their story shines like veins of gold
Through times that could not be foretold
For those who strove and those who fell
God bless this land they loved so well

The Homesteaders - Reflections

Epilogue

About the author

Julian Ashbourn is an accomplished author and landscape photographer who is known mostly for his non-fiction scientific works, covering both the natural science and technology fields.

The Homesteaders is his first novel, inspired by research originally undertaken into conservation in Canada, as reflected in the book In the Shadow of Inspiration. This volume is the third and last in a series which, together, provide an important chronicle of a particularly interesting period in the colourful history of Saskatchewan. It is hoped that this work helps to keep alive a story which is as rich in its humanity as it is in its history. It is a story which should not be forgotten as we rush, headlong, into the 21st century.

Julian Ashbourn lives in England and may be contacted via the web site http://ashbourn.zzl.org

Epilogue

Printed in Great Britain
by Amazon